Siegfried and the Vikings

By Simon de Wulf

First Published in 2020 by Blossom Spring Publishing

ISBN 978-1-8380188-9-4
E: admin@blossomspringpublishing.com
W: www.blossomspringpublishing.com
Published in the United Kingdom.

Dedication

For Cheryl and her support and encouragement in the writing of this story.

Chapter One

Siegfried awoke with a start. The sun was shining in through the window around the edges of the scrap of leather that covered it. It was time he went down to the river to fetch water for his mother.

He left their round house, a simple timbered dwelling covered in thatch, and began to make his way through the thick mist which hung over the pasture that bordered the River Uds. Above the mist it was a fine day with sparrows chattering in the branches of the thick bushes that bordered their property.

If Siegfried was tall enough he could probably see over the mist but he knew his way to the river blindfolded.

The year was 100 BC and Siegfried's village lay under a chalk cliff on the edge of a river that wound its way down to the sea not many miles away. He was of the Regni, a Celtic tribe who inhabited the south coast of Britain. As always he took a knife with him tucked into his belt, not that he needed it for protection as no marauders had visited their village for many years. But settlements close to the sea attracted pirates and sea borne vagrants often enough to ensure that every villager was warned to keep a look out and take care.

Apart from bad men, the elders of the village took delight in frightening the youngsters with tales of dragons, hydras, sea monsters, serpents and mystical beings that inhabited the wilder reaches of the countryside. Not that Siegfried, nor the other boys of the village, listened too much to their tales.

As Siegfried walked along whistling to himself he thought he heard a sound. He stood still. Suddenly, a great red and gold dragon with a fearsome stare loomed out of the mist above his head, not many yards from where he stood. Siegfried, frightened, dropped his wooden bucket and ran back to the house as fast as he could.

'Father, father, come quickly,' he shouted.

'Siegfried, what is it lad?' asked his father, noticing with worry that Siegfried's face was white with shock.

'A dragon father, down on the river. It's coming this way,' cried Siegfried.

'Steady lad, steady. Did you notice anything else?' asked his father taking hold of Siegfried by the arm. Siegfried calmed himself and thought for a moment.

'Yes. There was a splashing sound. That's what I heard. That's all.'

His father was silent for several seconds.

'Wait here,' he said as he went back inside their home. Moments later he emerged, buckling on an iron sword that had belonged to his father, and his father before him.

'Come with me,' he said.

Minutes later they entered the village and made straight for the largest house at its centre. It was the home of their chief, Drustan, a large, barrel chested man with a thick black beard now flecked with grey; a warrior who with his ten swordsmen provided protection to the settlement. Sitting on an upended bole of wood outside the main entrance was one of these men, who rose to his feet at their arrival.

'Hold hard Oengus, what's the rush?' asked the man belching loudly while he stretched his arms above his head.

'Fetch Drustan immediately,' commanded Oengus. 'And be quick about it!'

The man blinked in surprise but to Siegfried's astonishment he turned around and went straight inside. Drustan emerged moments later.

'Morning Oengus. What brings you to my door at this early hour?'

'Pirates my lord, on the river. We haven't a moment to lose.'

Drustan looked hard at Oengus for a moment before turning to the man who had been on watch outside his hall.

'Bricus, wake the men. I want them armed and down by the river in three minutes. Then round up the rest of the men in the village, as quickly and as quietly as you can.'

Within ten minutes, Drustan and his men plus several bleary eyed villagers were gathered in front of the pier that stretched out into the mist over the river. The villagers bore an assortment of weapons and the odd shield. But they stood in an organised line with Drustan's men making up the centre, with their shields hung on their left arms and swords in their right hands. No-one spoke. A thin man, the village baker, who sniffed constantly, finally broke the silence.

'Are you sure this isn't a false alarm my lord? I have bread baking and it will be burnt to a crisp unless I return to it,' he complained.

'Burnt bread will be the least of our worries,' growled Drustan, 'if what Oengus tells me is true.'

They stood patiently in silence, not keen to incur Drustan's wrath, as the rising sun slowly burnt off the mist revealing more of the river.

As the river came into view the men gasped. Sitting low on the water about thirty yards away was a craft the like of which none of them had seen before; a long, low wide vessel with straked woodwork culminating in a prow that bore the dragon's head that Siegfried had seen. It was a thing of beauty though deadly looking and threatening.

The men on board were just as deadly looking and

threatening. Covered in chain mail and all wearing swords, with some hefting wicked looking battleaxes, were some forty men. The largest was a giant, well over six feet tall with a mane of blonde hair and wearing a cloak of the brightest blue Siegfried had ever seen.

Both groups of men gazed at each other for several moments, before Drustan spoke first.

'I don't know who you are, but you are not welcome. Now turn your vessel around and head back out to sea, there is nothing for you here,' he shouted.

The blonde giant turned to a much smaller man who was stood next to him. He was unlike the others in that he wore no armour nor bore any weapons. It was he who responded in a form of Celtic that the men on the shore could understand.

'We come in peace. We only wish to trade and be allowed to beach our boat for repairs. We were caught up in a great storm at sea but by Odin's good grace were spared from Ran and her daughters when the storm lifted and showed us the river up which we have come.'

'A likely story,' commented one of Drustan's men

quietly.

'We do not wish to trade and your vessel looks sea worthy enough to me,' barked Drustan.

'My lord, we wish no harm. May I come ashore alone and unarmed and give you a token of our good faith?'

Before Drustan could respond, the man turned away, picked up a leather bag and leapt over the side of the boat. He swam swiftly to the shore keeping the bag above his head.

Several of Drustan's men drew their swords.

'Easy men, easy, put your swords away,' commanded Drustan. 'One unarmed man will cause no harm. Let's see what he brings us and what he has to say.'

The man emerged from the river, shaking the water off himself. He came up to Drustan and proffered the bag. Under the watchful eyes of his men, he undid it and withdrew the finest goblet they had ever seen. It was of red gold and adorned with several precious stones. The villagers had never seen an item of such value. It would feed the village for a year and then some.

'I knew it,' cried one of villagers. 'Pirates, how else

would they have come by such a thing?'

Drustan looked keenly at the wet man.

'Your story better be good,' he said.

'This was a gift to my Lord from a King up in the north of the country for a service he and his men rendered,' said the man. 'It is yours if you let us come ashore and make repairs to our boat and provide us with food, drink and supplies.'

Drustan took the proffered vessel and examined it carefully.

'Fine work; but what kind of service would you have provided for such a valuable prize?' he asked.

'My Lord is called Odo, the dragon slayer. Perhaps you have heard of him?' responded the man.

'Can't say that I have,' replied Drustan as he hefted the goblet in his big hand. The men crowded round for a better look.

'Mochan, what do you make of this?' asked Drustan as he handed the goblet to a portly looking man who was better dressed than the others.

'A chalice fit for a king, my Lord,' was his reply as he

examined the goblet with a greedy look. 'Red gold tells me it could come from Wales.'

'No doubt its origin is Welsh but it was the property of Pengar of the Parisi,' a deep voice said in a language no-one understood.

The men spun round to find themselves looking up at a tall, broad shouldered, muscular, god-like figure with long flaxen coloured hair. Unarmed and standing before them in a leather jerkin and cross laced breeches was the figure with the blue cloak from the striking looking ship.

There was a gasp and a rasp of steel as Drustan's men once again drew their swords.

Unnoticed by Drustan and his men, the man had slipped over the side of his ship and swum ashore. Drustan was shaken by his failure to keep an eye on the ship while questioning the small man who had brought the goblet. Things could have gone horribly wrong if several of the intruders had come ashore armed.

'May I introduce my lord Odo, the dragon slayer,' said the small man.

The men of the Regni looked uneasily at Odo and Drustan.

'Osric, tell him I come in peace and that we intend no harm. I am unarmed and wish to talk with black beard here; who I assume is their leader.'

Osric relayed Odo's words to Drustan.

'You are called Osric?' asked Drustan.

'Yes, my lord. I am a Gaulish trader from Samarobriva. I met Odo and his men in Gaul and they offered me passage to the country north of here, an unknown land of mists and forests. I speak their language and saw an opportunity to widen my trade. In return I was to act as an interpreter. The exchange suited us both.'

'You are either a brave or foolish man, Osric, to travel with such wild looking men. They have treated you well?'

'They have my lord. Odo is no pirate. He is a man of honour and has a story to tell which perchance you may care to hear at some point.'

'Maybe, maybe, but I need time to consult with the elders of my village. In the meantime, we will supply you with some food and drink and ask that you remain aboard your vessel while we deliberate in council. A boat will be provided to take you back to your ship.'

Osric relayed the gist of the conversation to Odo, who smiled briefly.

'The answer better be yes, Osric. I'm tired, hungry and so are the men. I see nothing here that frightens me. They better come to the right decision or I will make the decision for them and decide the outcome in our favour,' said Odo, suddenly looking grim.

'We gratefully receive your kind offer my lord,' said Osric turning to Drustan, though Drustan didn't for one moment believe that was the meaning of the exchange between the two men.

A small boat was fetched and one of Drustan's men rowed Odo and Osric back to their sleek craft.

Drustan detailed five of his men to stay on the pier to keep a watchful eye on the intruders, while he and the others set off for his hall where, once the village elders had gathered, they would discuss what was to be done.

Siegfried had been observing this exchange from the

shelter of one of the dwellings nearest the shore with several other boys. He was in awe of the flaxen haired giant and thought he looked like the kind of hero god that was woven into the folk tales recounted around their hearth fires.

As the men moved off to Drustan's house, his father among them, Siegfried followed at a distance, determined to find a way into the hall to listen to what was going to be discussed.

Chapter Two

The meeting of the council of elders had just begun by the time Siegfried managed to worm his way in under a bench at the back of the hall. This was a meeting for the adults of the village and the younger men of the community were not permitted to attend. But Siegfried's older sister was one of the women who had been tasked with serving refreshment to the men of the council and she had reluctantly agreed to smuggle Siegfried into the hall.

To Siegfried's surprise his father had been the first to be asked to take the floor and give his view.

'My lord and members of the Council, I suggest we welcome these barbarians to our village. I have heard of this Odo and what I have heard is favourable. When I was in the service of the Morini in Gaul, their chief hired Odo to rid his kingdom of a beast so terrible that men feared to go abroad about their daily business. Odo and his men slaughtered the monster and secured the respect and undying gratitude of the Morini.'

'That maybe Oengus, but Drustan has never

heard of him and if we don't show a strong hand and repel these marauders word will spread and, before we know it, every pirate and vagabond sailing these waters will know there are easy pickings among the Regni,' said a stout, florid faced man.

'We could proffer mead aplenty. These barbarians like their drink and then at the moon's turn we could slip out in several boats and slaughter them in their cups,' ventured the village's brewer.

'We could delay them with more food and drink and send word to Cadeyrn, our overlord, who would bring his hearth troop and see off these brigands,' said a pock faced man who smelt heavily of urine, used in his trade as tanner.

Oengus stood up once more. 'The facts are these. Facing us are Vikings, forty or more heavily armed men and every one a trained killer. Whether we like it or not, they could choose to come ashore at any time, kill without mercy all those of us who stand against them, take the remainder of our men and women as slaves and raze the village to the ground. Do you want to take that risk? We would be no match for them in close combat. Have no doubt, that as honourable a man as Odo may be, he will get what he wants.'

The debate went on for some time as every village elder ventured his view. During these exchanges Drustan kept silent and his face betrayed no emotion. Finally, when everyone present had spoken it was left to Drustan to take the floor.

'Thank you all for your council. I see that that the majority of you favour ridding ourselves of these barbarians. But whether we like it or not they represent a real threat to our community. I believe there is a way we can make their presence work to our advantage. I will let you know my decision shortly. Meanwhile, go about your daily business.'

Amid much grumbling the council broke up and the elders left the hall.

'Oengus, stay behind,' requested Drustan.

As the hall emptied Siegfried slipped away unobserved and returned home excited. Nothing like this has happened in his short life.

His father arrived shortly afterwards. Siegfried looked up at him.

'Father, what was the outcome?'

'I fear for the outcome, but Drustan is a sensible and pragmatic man and he will do what is right.'

'What's that father?' asked Siegfried.

'We'll know soon enough,' his father replied. 'Now go about your chores.'

Siegfried had wanted to ask his father, to all outward appearances a simple farmer, when he had served with the Morini and in what capacity. Clearly he had once been a warrior who was respected. This was all new to Siegfried but to ask would have betrayed his presence in the hall. With many questions in his head Siegfried left the house.

**

Drustan and his men gathered around the pier, every one in chain mail and bearing shield, spear and sword. Ten other men from the village who owned similar weaponry, Siegfried's father among them, joined the group. Twenty armed men putting on a show of strength for those warriors in the longship.

A small boat was sent out to fetch Osric, who scrambled aboard and came willingly ashore. Once aground, Drustan addressed him.

'Osric, we are not a barbarous people. We live in peace. But, make no mistake; we will defend what is ours, to the death if necessary. And should we all die many of your comrades will perish also.' Drustan looked directly at Osric while his men drummed their spears on their shields and uttered a low growl that was melodic in its rendition.

Osric stood his ground and returned Drustan's gaze. Drustan continued.

'We will welcome your companions on two conditions. The first is that your leader swears an oath that he will leave our village in peace. The second is that he will swear fealty to me as chief of the Leonids of the Regni and act as protector of our village for as long as we afford them a haven here. If they agree to these conditions I will let them beach their boat on the isle you see in the middle of the river. There they can make their repairs. We will supply them with food and any materials they need. Finally, they will remain on this island and not attempt to come ashore. We will ferry out to them whatever it is they need.'

'I will need to heed Odo's advice on this my lord,' replied Osric.

'No doubt,' said Drustan.

Osric was rowed out to the big ship on the water where a heated discussion took place observed by the men on the shore.

A dark, striking looking man was giving his opinion in no uncertain manner.

'Swear fealty to these scum? I would rather piss on our gods and give myself to Ran. I say we should take our ship into the pier and finish this. We do not need to abase ourselves to these fishermen.'

A couple of others grunted their agreement in support of the dark man.

'Violence is not always the path to follow Ingvar,' said a large red haired man standing beside Odo. Though shorter than Odo, he appeared almost as wide as he was tall with a huge barrel chest and stomach to match. His upper arms looked like they had been hewn from oak and were the size of most men thighs.

'I agree with Ingvar,' said a dark faced wiry man called Rolf. 'They may be fisherman and farmers but the village looks prosperous and the women look fair. We've been at sea a long time and need some entertainment.'

'Aye,' said another who could have been Rolf's twin. 'We will appear weak if we agree to black beard's plan.'

A handful of others supported this view. Several of the men echoed the large red haired man's observation and the discussion continued for some while until almost every man had his say. One man, considerably older than the rest, had not spoken. Odo turned to him.

'What do you say Uncle?' asked Odo.

The man in question stood and looked at every man aboard the longship before he spoke.

'May I remind you of why we are here and the oath we took before we left our homeland.

'We shall henceforth be men, at peace and pledged, at ale and eating, at gatherings, folk-meets and in a king's hall, and wherever men gather together we shall share both steel and meat and all things like friends and not like foes. And if, later, strife arises it shall be settled by peaceful means, with no swords reddened, but that one of you who is traitor to this truce and goes against word given, he shall become outlaw hunted and hated, so far as men ever an outlaw hunt.'

Silence descended on the longship. Those who had advocated violence looked down and shuffled their feet, all except Ingvar who looked at the grey bearded man with something close to contempt.

'Thorvald does well to remind us of our oath and why we set sail on the green seas,' said Odo. 'We need to make repairs to our craft. We are out of supplies. We are tired and need rest. Our quarrel is not with peaceful, law abiding men. If it's blood you want, there will be plenty in the months ahead. We will leave this village in peace. And I will agree to afford this settlement our protection while we are here. We need a base on this green and fertile land and this place gives us good shelter with easy access to the sea.'

The dark haired man, Ingvar, looked at Odo.

'Oath or no oath, we are wolves of the sea and as wolves we should decide what we take, when we take it and what we leave alone. We are outcasts. The elders of our people decided we should leave. We left not as ferocious and fearless men who value glory and valour above all things but as cowed dogs with our tails between our legs. I say it's time we take what we want, be bold and chart our own destiny that brings us riches and glory so we can return home with our heads held high,' said Ingvar, confronting Odo with his hand on his sword.

'Is that a challenge brother?' asked Odo.

'If it's a fight you want you can try me,' said the large red haired man.

'Stay out of this Arni. This is between me and my brother.'

'So, you assert your right to challenge for leadership of our band of brothers,' said Odo.

The entire Viking band went still. Viking leaders were appointed by consent through a democratic tradition that stretched back into time immemorial. It was the right of any man in the band to propose a new leader. If the majority supported the new leader, the existing leader made way for him. If only a few supported the new leader then he had the right to issue a challenge and make himself leader by force of arms. However, the majority among the crew supported Odo and both Odo and Ingvar knew this.

Ingvar stared at Odo for several seconds before he dropped his hand from his sword and smiled.

‘I’m not looking for a fight brother. As is my right I’m stating my point of view and hoping to make you see sense.’

‘I have listened Ingvar and my decision is that we leave these people in peace. Osric, tell the man in the boat that I will be but a few minutes. Arni, you will accompany me with Osric.’

Minutes later Odo, Arni and Osric boarded the boat. Odo was dressed as Siegfried had first seen him, in gleaming chain mail with his bright blue cloak fastened about his shoulders and with his sword buckled around his waist. Arni looked no less impressive in his full war gear, hefting a massive double headed axe that was his preferred choice of weapon.

The boat set out for the shore to where Drustan and his men waited.

'So, you have reached a decision Odo?' asked Drustan.

'I have Drustan. We will abide by your terms. I will leave your village in peace and I and my men will swear fealty to you as chief of the Leonids of the Regni and will act as protector of your village for as long as we are welcome here.'

Osric translated.

'Kneel then Odo of the Vikings and place your hands between mine and repeat your oath.'

Odo knelt and repeated the oath. He then got to his feet and Drustan grasped him high on his left forearm with his right hand.

'We extend a welcome to you and your men. To seal this oath we will hold a feast tomorrow night at which you all will be welcome.'

Odo, Arni and Osric made their way back to the boat and set out for their longship.

'Let's beach our craft and get to work,' said Odo to Arni and Osric.

Chapter Three

The crew of the longship carefully navigated their boat towards the island that had been designated for them in the middle of the river. Propelled by oars the men drove the boat hard up onto the soft shore. Two of the crew leapt overboard with the anchor and almost immediately disappeared up to their thighs in mud. With much difficulty they extricated themselves, pushed the anchor into the mud and set off to explore the small piece of land. Minutes later one of them returned and shouted out to Odo who was standing at the prow.

'This haven is no good my lord; nothing but a swamp full of flies with no hard standing.'

Ingvar, who had heard the man's remark, was quick with his comment.

'I knew we couldn't trust these Celts. I say we return to the village and show them just what we think of our side of the agreement.'

'Hold hard Ingvar,' said Odo. 'Arni, reverse rowing positions and pull us towards their pier.'

Two of Drustan's men, who had been left on guard on

the river bank, watched in consternation as the longship reversed its direction of travel and moved towards the pier. Siegfried was standing close by.

'Boy, fetch Drustan and the rest of the men immediately,' the older of the two commanded. Siegfried raced off at once into the centre of the village.

By the time the longship came to rest, Drustan and the rest of his men were drawn up along the end of the pier.

'What is this?' asked Drustan, as Odo and Osric jumped down onto the pier.

'That island is a swamp, fit only for flies and birds. We cannot beach our ship and repair it there. We need to bring our ship onto the bank this side of the river, onto dry ground with ready access to facilities,' said Osric.

Before Drustan could answer, a high pitched cackle greeted Osric's rely. An old man with penetrating eyes dressed in white robes with long white hair and a long white beard stepped forward.

'Solve a riddle and we will grant you landing rights,' he said.

Osric looked at the figure that hadn't been present when they first landed. If he wasn't mistaken the man was a Druid, a member of the Celtic religious cast whose spiritual home was in Anglesey, an island off the Welsh coast. Revered by the Celtic peoples these men were their spiritual guardians, men of wisdom and insight, healers, dreamers and soothsayers. Many thought they were the living embodiment of their gods, able to interpret through their dreams what their gods wanted. They were respected and feared in equal measure.

'What do you mean old man?' asked Drustan.

'I have communed with the spirits who foretold of these strangers arrival on our shores. To remain with us they have to satisfy our gods that they are worthy. They have tasked me with a riddle that needs to be solved.'

'And what may that riddle be?' asked Drustan.

'These strangers ask for access to our land. Macha, goddess of cunning, war, life, and death, she who wears a cloak woven of raven feathers, has set the task. She will grant the intruders land but only as much land as can be covered by the hide of one cow.'

As if to reinforce this vision, a pair of ravens, cawing loudly, circled overhead before settling themselves on one of the posts abutting the pier.

'You see, Macha has indeed spoken,' said the druid.

There was much muttering and crossing of arms among Drustan's men. Osric reached for a stone that was on a thong around his neck. Odo knew an ill omen when he saw one and touched the hilt of his sword in which was set a precious piece of amber from his home country.

'Osric what is the meaning of all this?' asked Odo.

Osric explained. Odo, not an overly religious man, knew better than to confront the wishes of the gods even though the god in question was not one of his.

'Tell Drustan we will give him an answer within the hour.' Turning on his heel, Odo walked back down the pier and returned to his ship.

Once on board he told Osric to keep his mouth shut and sought out Thorvald and a man called Aun who was their rune master, a mystic and fortune-teller who made the necessary sacrifices that were essential before they undertook all voyages, adventures and battles. He relayed the gist of what the druid had told him.

'A seemingly impossible riddle to solve,' said Thorvald.

'Maybe, maybe, give me time,' said Aun.

'We have an hour,' stated Odo, 'after which I may not be able to restrain Ingvar and the others.

Aun left them and returned with a cloak made of bear skin which he laid out on the deck. He reached into a satchel and drew out a number of heavily inscribed bones which he laid down on the cloak. He asked for a bowl of hot water which was brought and placed alongside the bones and into which he deposited shavings from what looked like a stick of resin. These began to give off a not unpleasant smell. Aun leant over the bowl and inhaled deeply and slowly went into a trance. He began to mutter various phrases and incantations which were unintelligible to Odo and Thorvald. The rest of the Viking band watched from a distance having been told that Aun was consulting with the Gods on what course of action would be favourable.

Well used to Aun's ways they were content to await the outcome.

After several minutes Aun cast the bones in the air and watched them land on the bear skin. He examined them closely. His head bowed over the bones and he appeared to have fallen asleep. After what seemed an eternity he stood up, stripped naked and jumped over the side of the ship into the river. He emerged from the waters and climbed back on board. He sluiced the water off himself, towelled himself down before donning his breeches and jerkin.

He looked up at Odo and Thorvald and gave them his considered view on how they should proceed. Odo smiled broadly and smacked him on the arm.

'Come Thorvald, let's see what the Celts make of this,' he said as he jumped back over the side of the ship onto the pier.

'Drustan, we accept your offer. Bring us the hide of a cow and show us the land we can spread it on,' said Odo. Osric translated.

Drustan looked bemused.

'Very well,' he said and gave the necessary order.

The newly cured hide of a cow was duly fetched and given to Odo who took possession of it. Drustan then asked Odo and Osric to follow him upstream to a meadow that was north of the village. It abutted the river and was an ideal piece of land on which to draw up their craft and make camp.

'We will return to our ship and meet you here later when we are ready,' said Odo.

'So be it,' replied Drustan, curious to know how Odo and his men planned to solve the puzzle set them by the druid.

Once back on board the longship, Aun set to work.

Some time later the longship pulled slowly alongside the shore. Odo, Osric and Aun stepped ashore. Aun held a bundle in his arms.

'Drustan, we have come to claim the land you have promised us. Aun, lay out the cow skin,' commanded Odo.

Aun stepped forward with a shapeless mass. He leant over and pegged a piece of what looked like a ball of leather string into the ground. He then set off from the shore unravelling the ball of string as he went. He walked around in a circle pegging the string at intervals into the earth. By the time he had finished he had covered an area of meadow that was large enough to take the longship and provide room enough for a tented encampment.

'What trickery is this?' asked Drustan.

'No trickery,' replied Osric on behalf of Odo, 'You will see that the twine we have used to demarcate our land is the cow skin, completely whole, but cut fine. We have spread it over the ground that you promised us.'

'It is not complete,' replied Drustan.

'But it is,' said Osric, 'there are no breaks in the hide.

'The hide had to remain whole and not be cut,' said Drustan.

'You made no such condition my lord,' said Osric.

Drustan turned to the druid, who had been watching proceedings carefully. He burst out laughing and shook his head.

'They have the better of you Drustan. They have

solved the riddle in an imaginative way. Their gods must favour them and Macha will approve of their cunning. Their god Loki, the shape shifter, must have come to them to show them the way.'

Are you saying we must accept this interpretation of the riddle,' asked Drustan.

'Aye, my lord, we must, otherwise we will anger the spirits.' replied the druid.

'It seems you have your land. But no straying from this meadow unless invited or we give you permission,' said Drustan to Odo.

'On my oath,' replied Odo.

Chapter Four

The next day Siegfried awoke at the same time he always did. As he went down to the river to fetch water he thought about the events of the day before. He was fascinated by these large warriors from a land far away.

He had watched as they had come ashore on the meadow that been granted to them before being ushered away by one of Drustan's men. He wanted to get close to them and have a look at their swords and battleaxes.

He knew that a feast was being prepared that evening for the Viking band and that all had been invited. He must speak with his sister to see if he could gain access to the hall for the evening's festivities.

Meanwhile, he had to run a number of errands. He had to barter for bread and meat and some other things for his mother.

On the way back from the baker's he noticed Mochan, the merchant, acting suspiciously in a side alley behind a large round hut that served as his warehouse. He was speaking with four of his men, natural thugs who acted as protectors of his convoys and body guards to him.

On impulse, Siegfried slipped into a cow byre next to the warehouse and pressed himself up against a loose wooden board that separated the two. He could see through a gap between the boards and hear quite clearly what Mochan was now saying to the men, who he had invited inside.

'It must be done tonight. The barbarians will all be at the feast and no doubt fully in their cups when the moon is at its highest. You must strike then. Forget the individual chests belonging to the men. Find their main treasure chest and take it before you set fire to their boat. You must make it look like an accident. They will no doubt have left a fire-pot on board. It may not be fully alight but it will contain embers. Tip this pot over and make it look like the embers have caused the fire. Have you got that?' Mochan asked.

'Yes sir,' was the surly reply from the largest of the men.

'And arrange for my horse and cart to be ready for

departure straight after your return. We leave for my cousin's village. It's going to be a clear night so we should see our way readily enough.'

The men nodded and Mochan rubbed his hands together briskly before dismissing them.

Siegfried was alarmed by this treachery. These Vikings had come in good faith. He wanted to get to know them and now his plan was in jeopardy because of the greed of Mochan the merchant. And who knows what trouble would be caused when the Vikings, full of drink, realised that their precious craft had been burnt to a cinder. They would kill everyone in the village.

With that thought Siegfried raced home to give his purchases to his mother. Without waiting for a reply he ran out of the house and set off through the fields behind their home towards the dense tree line that bordered the base of the chalk cliff behind their village. He knew the woodland trails backwards and had learnt to move silently through the forest. Within a short period of time he had worked his way northwards through the trees until he came to rest behind an oak tree opposite the meadow in which the Vikings had berthed their craft.

It was late morning and he could see various parties of men at work de-scaling the underside of the boat while others had begun to saw up logs to make planks of wood to replace the damage done to the long clinkered boards that made up the surface structure of the longship.

Siegfried wondered how best to proceed when he heard a twig snap and then felt something heavy strike the back of his neck. He passed out immediately.

The next thing he felt was a bucket of water being thrown over his face. The effect was instantaneous. He immediately sat up spluttering.

'So what have we here?' a voice asked in passable Celtic.

'I need to speak with your chief,' spat out Siegfried.

'You do, do you little cub?' said the man.

'Who are you?' asked Siegfried.

'I am known as Aun, though many call me Vili because of my wit and intelligence. Vili is brother to Odin, the

Allfather, and I see that they have sent you to me. I told Odo only last night that we need to make sacrifice and within hours the gods have delivered you to me. This makes my day.'

'Take no notice of him,' said another man who cuffed Aun lightly around the head. 'I am Arni and you are lucky that it was my cousin Asbjorn who came across you skulking in the trees. We do not like spies and it could have gone ill for you if Ingvar or one of his followers had come across you, despite the fact that you are little more than a boy. So, what is it that brings you into our encampment for make no mistake this meadow and the fringe of trees yonder are now Viking territory?'

Siegfried was amazed that the Vikings spoke Celtic, albeit badly. He had thought only Osric knew their tongue.

'I have come to warn you of a terrible deed that will befall you and your men this evening,' blurted out Siegfried. He then recounted what he had heard.

Arni looked at him, nodded and said he would be back in a moment. He returned with Odo and Thorvald and asked Siegfried to repeat what he had told him. Siegfried looked up in awe at three of the biggest and, at the same time, most frightening men he had seen in his life and repeated his tale.

'You have done well boy,' said Odo, 'now take this and return to your people without a word of what has been said here. Do you understand?

'Yes, my lord' said Siegfried.

Odo had given Siegfried a silver coin of Gaulish design. It would pay for many meals for Siegfried's family. Clutching it tightly Siegfried was escorted to the trees before being let go. He disappeared almost immediately into the undergrowth without a sound.

'That boy would make an excellent scout,' remarked Arni, 'Now we have plans to make.'

**

There was a buzz of excitement in the village as the time for the feast drew near. It was not often a feast was held. The smell of roasting beef and pork wafted from the kitchens attached to Drustan's hall. Serving women cleaned the long trestle tables and laid out wooden plates and goblets for the mead that was sure to be drunk to excess that night.

Just as the sun began to set, Odo and his band arrived outside the hall escorted by two of Drustan's men. While not in chain mail they all wore their swords. Drustan greeted them at the main door to the hall.

'Welcome Odo to our humble hall. Before we go in I must ask that you leave your swords outside. I will have no weapons in my hall on a feast night.'

Odo turned to his men and requested they remove their swords. Several of the men were not happy at this, particularly Ingvar.

'I hope you know what you are doing brother. This won't be the first time strangers have suffered at the hands of Celtic treachery.'

'Do as I say Ingvar. We are guests here and we outnumber their fighting men. Should there be treachery here we will be more than a match for them with our bare hands. Besides which we will have the knives that we eat with.'

Ingvar grunted but unbuckled his sword and gave it to

one of Drustan's men who stockpiled the weapons outside the hall door under a wooden lean to.

Siegfried had arranged for himself to be present at the feast as a kitchen boy helping to carry the great haunches of cooked meats into the hall to be placed on the tables for those present. His sister and several other womenfolk were tasked with bringing the mead and keeping the diners goblets full of the sweet, golden liquid.

Drustan sat at the head of the table with Odo at his right hand and Osric next to him to act as translator. At his left side was his wife Briaca, a handsome looking woman with dark lustrous hair held back at each side with clasps containing jewels that caught and reflected the candle light. The rest of the women folk were sat at a separate table lower down the hall. Odo's men were alternately sat between the male men of the settlement. Drustan felt this would minimise any likely trouble whether through drink or devilry. At least four of Drustan's men took no part in the feast and wore their swords. Two stood behind Drustan against the end wall of the hall with the other two either side of the immense doorway that, seemingly, was the only entry and exit from the hall. As far as Drustan could see, all of Odo's warriors were present in the hall though this wasn't the case.

Two Vikings, fully armed and in chain mail, had positioned themselves in a cow byre opposite the hall. At the first sign of trouble they were to secure the band's weapons and, if necessary, fight their way into the hall and ensure as many swords as possible were distributed to Odo and his men. Two others had remained with their longship.

Arni had taken a place on the bench nearest the door and found himself sandwiched between Mochan the trader and the village's brewer. A sheen of perspiration coated Mochan's face.

'You look warm brother?' said Arni in his poor Celtic. Mochan looked surprised.

'So, you speak Celtic then?' replied Mochan.

'Aye, most of us do. We have spent time among the Morini and the Bellovaci of Gaul. We are not as fluent as

Osric, but we get by.'

'Was that mercenary work?' asked Mochan, 'for you do not appear to be traders.'

'No brother, traders we are not. We are on a mission to claim glory and to claim that glory through ridding the lands we visit of monsters, dragons and serpents that bring terror and pestilence to good honest folk like yourselves,' Arni replied with a smile while clapping Mochan on the back with his large hand.

Mochan laughed uneasily.

Odo, meanwhile, was making small talk with Drustan. As he spoke, Siegfried placed a platter of bread rolls in front of them. As he turned away he looked at Odo who winked and smiled at him. Drustan's wife noticed the exchange.

'You know this boy?' asked Drustan's woman.

'Nay my lady, how could I, but he seems a fine and upright lad.'

'He is that,' she replied. 'His father was once a warrior of renown before deciding to forsake arms and seek a peaceable existence as a farmer.'

'A warrior's path is not for every man. Indeed, I often think the world would be a better place if we could all live in peace with one another,' said Odo wistfully.

'So, we have a warrior who would be a peace maker among us,' said Drustan who had been listening to the conversation.

'We cannot always choose our calling or the journey our gods set for us, though I often wish it otherwise,' said Odo.

Drustan was keen to understand what had brought Odo and crew into their waters and moved the conversation in this direction.

Chapter Five

The moon was at its zenith in the sky when Mochan's men moved silently towards the outline of the longship. All was quiet and no watch seemed to have been set. The sky was clear and the half-moon shone down making it easy for the approaching men to see where they were going.

Apart from the longship, the area around it contained an assortment of material, work benches which contained wooden planks ready for finishing, barrels of water and other supplies, bales of hay, and a leather tent that appeared to contain an assortment of shipwrights' tools. The men hesitated as these afforded good cover for any waiting and vigilant guard.

The four men stood stock still, sniffed the air and carefully examined the barrels and bales of hay before checking out the inside of the tent. Satisfied, they picked their way carefully towards the side of the craft.

As they stood below the longship, their leader issued instructions quietly. Two of the men were to remain beside the ship, one at each end, while the other two climbed on board to begin the task of finding the ship's main treasure chest before setting fire to the craft.

The two men left on guard separated and moved off to either end of the longship. As the man at the end nearest the shore reached his position he thought he heard the long grass rustle. As he began to turn towards the sound a hand clamped itself over his mouth and the last thing he felt was a massive blow to the side of his head. It was enough to lay him out flat and unconscious. The man at the other end was dealt with in the same way. Both men were then gagged with their arms bound tightly. Leather thongs were also applied to their ankles restricting their movement.

'Good work Finn,' whispered Geir, the other Viking left behind on watch at the ship, 'now for the two on board.'

Finn and Geir approached one of the prows of the ship, the craft's highest point where a rope ladder had been fixed. They shinned up the ladder silently. They wore only their breeches with knives in their teeth to reduce noise. They were relying on surprise.

Unlike Mochan's men, they knew their way around every inch of the ship. They moved forward silently until they could see the two men bending over a large chest trying to prise the lid open. The lock gave and both men lifted the lid. They gasped as the moon light shone down on the gold and silver ornaments and coins it contained.

'Our master will be well pleased,' the larger of the two said. It was the last words he uttered. Geir took him and Finn the other. They had left heavy lump hammers on board and with these knocked the pair unconscious. They swiftly bound and gagged them before heaving them up and dropping them unceremoniously over the side.

'Thor favours the brave,' said Finn.

'And Loki favours those with cunning,' said Geir, 'now let's wake them up. We need to work swiftly.'

Both men dropped to the ground, picked up the inert forms of the men and placed them side by side. They retrieved two buckets of water which they promptly threw over the four men. All four gradually came to, shaking their heads and moaning through their gags.

'Steady men, steady,' said Geir.

They got all four men to their feet and connected them together with a single piece of rope. Prodding them with the points of their swords they guided them in the direction of the village.

The feast was in full swing as the party of six slipped quietly through the outer settlements of the village looking for Mochan's yard, the location of which had been described by Siegfried.

**

Inside the feasting hall Mochan was sweating freely and feeling giddy with the effects of the mead Arni was ensuring he drank copious amounts of.

'Another toast to our good fortune that we met you Leonids of the Regni,' said Arni, clashing his wooden goblet against that of Mochan's which sounded empty.

'Wench, bring more mead here for this good man of the Regni,' shouted Arni to a passing village girl who bore a jug of the golden liquid.

'No, no more,' cried Mochan.

'What, you will not share a toast with your new found

friends,' said Arni menacingly. 'You will dishonour me if you do not drink to our new alliance.'

'Come Mochan, relax and enjoy Drustan's mead. It's the best in the village,' said the village's brewer who sat on the other side of Arni.

'I should know, I brewed it,' he said giggling inanely.

Mochan had no choice but to comply. He was anxious for the feast to finish so he and his men could be well away from the village with the spoils from the Viking ship before they realised their loss. But everyone was enjoying themselves and the feast showed no signs of ending any time soon.

'I need to piss,' said Mochan attempting to get up from the bench. A huge hand grasped his arm.

'Stay where you are,' commanded Arni. 'You're going nowhere.'

Mochan looked around but no-one seemed to notice that he was being forcibly held down on his seat. Not a brave man, Mochan decided that compliance was the best policy.

'As you say red beard, let's have another toast.'

Mochan was not stupid and quickly realised that playing along was his only option. At some point the feast would finish and he'd be able to slip away before dawn even if he was groggy with mead.

Unfortunately for Mochan the feast continued until sunrise, at which point Drustan called a halt to proceedings. Many of the men, Vikings included, were already slumped over the tables asleep, full of food and alcohol.

Odo, Arni and those of the Vikings who still seemed fairly fresh gathered up their drunken comrades and left for their encampment.

Mochan bustled away as quickly as he could towards his yard. He had to get away before his crime was uncovered.

As he tottered towards his dwelling Siegfried, who had taken no part in the drinking or feasting, followed at a discreet distance.

As Mochan entered his yard Siegfried heard him cry out in alarm. Siegfried hastily followed. What met his eyes was a sight to behold. As well as being a merchant,

Mochan was a slave trader. He dealt in captives taken from neighbouring tribes and selling captives as slaves was a profitable business. The wealthier families of the village had many slaves working their fields or undertaking house work.

Standing in his yard was a slave wagon, a cart with four wheels containing a wooden cage. Inside this cage were Mochan's men, bound and gagged and looking sheepish. Mochan was frantically trying to undo the rope that bound the cage door to release his men. He was beside himself with fury.

'Ninian you fool, what have you done? I set you a simple task and you have fouled up. I will see you all pay for this,' cried Mochan who, unable to untie the rope, disappeared inside his dwelling to return with a large knife.

Siegfried slipped away before he was noticed. A potential crisis had been averted and he was eager to return to the Viking camp to update them on this turn of events and to hear what had happened.

**

Siegfried slipped away through the trees behind the village and set off in the direction of the Viking camp. This time there was no-one keeping watch in the tree line to surprise him. He approached the ship and ran into Asbjorn.

'So, young man it seems we owe you our thanks. I'll fetch Odo.'

Siegfried stood in the shadow of the longship as Odo approached from the direction of the leather tent.

'You have done well boy. We caught the men and returned them to Mochan's yard. I don't think they will be troubling us again. Now, how I can I repay you for the help you have given us?'

'I'd like to be a Viking and learn how to fight like you,' said Siegfried. 'Would you teach me?'

'Hmm, that depends on your father. Would he be happy to know that you are among us picking up our ways?'

'I don't know but I can ask. Perhaps I can suggest to him that I help you repair your ship and carry out other tasks. In return you can show me how to use a sword and the axe.'

Odo laughed. 'The sword we can certainly show you but the axe requires great strength and skill. And I think you are not yet grown enough for that weapon. How old are you?'

'Thirteen,' replied Siegfried.

'Thirteen?' repeated Odo. 'Speak with your father and we'll see what can be done.'

Siegfried set off reluctantly back to the village. His father was with Drustan.

'Father, I must speak with you.'

'Not now boy. I'm busy.'

'Let the boy speak,' said Drustan.

'I want to help the Vikings and learn their ways, I'd like to be a warrior like them.'

His father sighed. 'A warrior's life is hard and full of danger Siegfried. It is not for everyone and as my eldest and only son you must look after our farm, your mother and your sister should something happen to me.'

'But father did you not tell me once that to defeat your enemies you must know them. Working with Odo and his men I will learn a lot about them.’

Drustan burst out laughing. ‘That sounds like you Oengus, full of wisdom as ever. The boy is right. We could do with a spy in their camp to tell us how they progress and what they are thinking.’

‘I don’t want to be a spy,’ said Siegfried shaking his head.

Drustan grabbed his arm in a vice like grip and looked hard at him, all traces of humour vanishing.

‘Now listen here boy. I will agree to you helping the barbarians, as will your father, on the condition that you keep us informed on what they are thinking and doing. Otherwise you will be confined to the village. Is that understood?’

Siegfried thought for a moment and nodded. After all what could there be to tell? The Vikings would repair their ship and leave.

‘I’ll do it,’ he said.

‘Good boy Siegfried. Come and see me at the end of every day and give me a report.’ With that Drustan turned away.

'Siegfried, beware, he who sups with the Devil should have a long spoon,' said his father.

'What does that mean?'

'It means you should take care.'

'I will father. I will.'

Chapter Six

The next four weeks sped by as the Vikings repaired their ship and recovered fully from their ordeal at sea. It was obvious to Siegfried that many of the Vikings were getting restless and were keen to leave and assume their quest for glory and riches.

Odo was as good as his word and every afternoon Arni, Asjborn and others showed Siegfried how to wield a sword. It was a wooden training sword, much to Siegfried's disgust, but it was heavier than a normal blade and built up strength in his arms and ensured that no-one was accidentally hurt in the combative drills he was put through.

At end of the four weeks Arni took Siegfried aside.

'You are doing well lad. It's time to find you a real blade. Come with me.'

Arni led Siegfried towards the leather tent that stood close by the ship.

Laid out inside the tent was the war gear of all the Vikings. Each piece had been cleaned and coated with mutton fat to keep the ever present rust at bay. The various swords and axes fascinated Siegfried. The sword that caught his immediate attention was a massive blade encased in a beautifully worked leather scabbard. The top of the hilt shone yellow in the light and seemed to sparkle.

'How about that one?' asked Siegfried pointing at the sword that had caught his eye.

'How about that one indeed!' replied Arni. 'That is Dragon Slayer and is a special weapon. That is Odo's sword and only he is entitled to wield it.'

'May I have a closer look at it, please,' pleaded Siegfried.

Arni took up the scabbard and withdrew the impressive sword. The blade was a clear misty blue grey with hardly any markings upon it except some letters chased in gold along its upper length near the handle.

Arni handed it to Siegfried who struggled with its weight. He sat down and laid it across his lap. He studied the letters which read 'Ulfberse'.

'What is the meaning of this?' asked Siegfried.

'That is the name of the man who made it. A famous

warrior he learnt his craft as a smith in lands far away from here. He was a baresark, a warrior who seeks single combat and fights in a violent frenzy with a skill that few can beat. He feels no pain and if he can't kill his opponent outright will wear him down through sheer force and stamina. No-one knows where he came from. Some say he was brought up by wolves hence his name Ulf, meaning wolf. Berse is short for Baresark or Beserker and so he is known as Ulfberse. It is said that whoever owns one of his swords will never be defeated in combat. It is a unique sword. It is strong and has a spirit that means the man who wields it can do so in complete confidence that it will never shatter and is easily retrieved from shields, chain mail and human flesh allowing him to always be ready for his next opponent.'

'How do you get hold of one of these magical swords?'

'To own one of these swords is down to Ulf. It then requires a special skill, passing a certain ritual and then a lot of gold.'

'What skill and what is a ritual?'

'You ask a lot of questions,' smiled Arni. 'You have to satisfy Ulf that you are warrior enough to wield one of his blades. To demonstrate your skill you have to fight him in combat. If he deems you worthy, and you have the gold to pay for it, he will make you one. Having said this, Ulf decides at the outset whether he will forge you a sword or not. The spirits speak to him and there is no gain saying his decision. There are many renowned warriors who would like such a sword and have the skill and the gold to pay for it but who Ulf deems not worthy enough.'

'Odo must be a special man.'

'He is that lad. He is one of the chosen ones.'

'Can anyone else make a sword like this? I'm sure Cathas, our smith, could make such a blade.'

'I doubt it lad. It takes many days, a special forge, secret techniques, and some magic to make such a blade. This sword was dipped in dragon's blood and Ulf is the only man I know who can make such a weapon.'

'Do you have such a sword?'

'Nay lad, I prefer the double headed axe. Few have

the strength or skill to use one and I wager that I will always defeat a warrior wielding a sword.'

Siegfried would dearly like to own such a sword as Odo's but realised that this was a dream. He looked wistfully at it as Arni returned it to its scabbard.

'Come on now. I have found just the blade for you. It is a cut down version fashioned for Thorvald's nephew, Karl, when he was your age.'

Getting up Siegfried took the sword he was given and followed Arni out of the tent.

'Now let's see what you can do with this,' said Arni as he led Siegfried towards a hefty wooden post that had been set well into the ground.

'Take your position and imagine that this post is a warrior who is facing you. Advance towards it and put into practice some of the drills we have taught you.'

Siegfried approached the post and took guard with his sword pointing out straight in front of him. He lunged toward the post with a straight arm and then brought his sword back before bringing it down in an arc towards the upper right hand side. He chipped off a flake of wood. He immediately retreated before scything in low at ankle height. He stepped back before reversing his blow towards the upper left part of the post before stepping back and then forward with an overhead swipe at the top of the post where his sword wedged itself and refused to be drawn back.

Arni burst out laughing. 'That is an occupational hazard young man. Now what would you do if that happened in combat?' he asked.

'I would retreat a step behind my shield and wait for an opportunity to retrieve it,' he said.

'Good, hopefully your fellow warriors in the shield wall would cover you while you then had another go at regaining it. It is bad luck to leave your blade stuck in the head of some barbarian warrior.'

Watching this practice was Rolf, who had his sword in his hand.

'Instead of a post, why don't you practice your new found skills against a real warrior,' he challenged.

'Rolf, get back to work. He is too green to come up against a seasoned swordsman.'

Siegfried's blood was up and he stepped forward to face Rolf. 'I can take him,' he cried.

Before Arni could prevent him, Siegfried lunged towards Rolf with his sword. His speed surprised Rolf who barely managed to step out of reach. Siegfried followed up with a cut to his shoulder before dropping back and attempting a slash at his thigh. Rolf, who had recovered his poise, parried the strokes as he stepped backwards.

'I'll say that for him but the lad is quick,' he said.

'Rolf, if you damage the lad you will have me to deal with' growled Arni.

Siegfried danced around Rolf putting into practice all he had learnt from Arni and the others. Rolf absorbed all of Siegfried's blows until he began to tire. Then without warning Rolf struck Siegfried across the upper arm with the flat of his blade and came in close striking Siegfried on the head with the butt of his sword. Siegfried collapsed to the ground.

Arni rushed forward. 'Rolf I warned you to take it easy.'

'It was but a light blow,' countered Rolf.

'If you're wrong, I'll gut you,' said Arni.

Arni cradled Siegfried's head in his hands. Rolf, bring me some mead.'

Rolf fetched a horn of mead which Arni forced between Siegfried's lips. He started to cough and splutter.

'Easy lad, easy,' said Arni. 'You have taken a blow to head and will feel groggy for a while.'

Siegfried came round and sat up.

'Now that was foolish. The second lesson in fighting is to keep a cool head. If you let emotion rule you, you will be undone. Don't get me wrong, emotion is a good thing. We all need the courage that anger and frustration can bring but you need to channel these emotions correctly. A rash fighter is a dead fighter. Do you understand me?'

Siegfried nodded.

'Good boy. You have the signs of becoming a good warrior. You have heart and are fast, faster than most, and when you grow into your strength and learn the skill of the Viking sword I venture you will become deadly but you need to keep a cool head. And that means learning to avoid idiot challenges from the likes of Rolf. Do you understand me?'

'Yes,' replied Siegfried.

'Good. Now that's enough for one day, time you went home,' said Arni clapping him on the shoulder affectionately.

With that Siegfried stumbled off towards the village.

Odo had been observing the exchange.

'Don't get too attached to him Arni. We will be leaving tomorrow.'

'Ah, he's good boy. I can't deny that he would be a son to be proud of. He works hard and is a keen learner. He would make a good Viking given time. I'll miss teaching him'

Siegfried and the Vikings - 'The Dragon's Lair'

Chapter Seven

It was early morning with mist covering the meadow where the Viking encampment lay in semi-darkness. The ground began to tremble and a sound like thunder filled the air.

Hakon, who was on watch, peered anxiously through the mist. He called out to the man who was on watch with him, his close friend and shield companion who sat next to him on the starboard side of their longship.

'Hastein, rouse Odo and the others, demons approach us.'

Looming out of the mist was a terrifying sight; huge war horses with faceless figures shrouded in leather and iron armour bearing shields and spears. For a moment Hakon thought the Valkyries had come for him deciding it was his time to be borne off to Valhalla, a hall for the slain ruled over by the god Odin in the afterlife. He gripped the amulet around his neck and offered up a quick prayer as the horses came to a halt some thirty yards from where he stood. As they came to a halt

Hastein realised the riders seated on the big chargers were men and he felt a little better. He and his companions could deal with men.

The group of mounted warriors looming over him became motionless with only their horses snorting and pawing the ground. It was a chilling sight.

Within minutes the Vikings, used to reacting to danger quickly, took up station alongside Hakon, their shields overlapping in a shield wall, swords and axes drawn.

Many of the Vikings touched their sacred talismans at the sight of these anonymous warriors wreathed in mist and seemingly unmoving.

'How many do you think?' asked Arni.

'Fifty at least,' replied Odo.

'Keep your shields up and locked together. Horses don't like a solid barrier,' said Odo addressing his men.

One of the riders, on a stallion as black as night, edged his mount away from the others towards the Viking band. He was an impressive figure, muscular and bare-chested with a yellow cloak fastened around his shoulders held by a huge ruby red broach set in gold and a heavy gold torc around his neck. His chest was covered in swirling blue tattoos. His head was framed with long black hair and on his arms were many warrior rings of gold.

'I am Cadeyrn, high chief of the Regni people. Who are you that occupy my land?'

Odo, no less an impressive figure than Cadeyrn, stepped forward. 'I am Odo, son of Sigurd, lord of the Skein, and known as Dragon slayer.'

'And what brings you to my lands?'

'Our ship suffered in a great storm and Drustan, chief of the Leonids of the Regni, afforded us safe haven to repair it and to provide us with the supplies we needed. In return we agreed to protect his village for as long as we are welcome here.'

Cadeyrn looked down on Odo.

'I am surprised that Drustan felt his village needed protection. The Regni are a people well used to fighting for their own and I afford all the protection they need.'

'Perhaps my lord, but the village is close to the sea

and some distance from your hearth and the seas contain all manner of pirates and marauders looking for easy plunder.'

'And you are not such as they?' asked Cadeyrn.

'Nay my lord, warriors we may be but pirates we are not.'

Cadeyrn looked directly at Odo for several seconds.

'We'll see. I will consult with Drustan. In the meantime I will leave a score of my men on the boundary of your camp.' With that, Cadeyrn turned his horse away and cantered off in the direction of the village followed by the rest of his hearth troop.

'I wonder what brings the high chief here,' said Thorvald to Odo and Arni.

'Whatever it is I don't much like it,' replied Arni.

'We'll know the answer soon enough,' said Odo as he pointed to a horseman coming back towards them from the village.

'You, and you alone, are requested to accompany me to the hall,' stated the horseman.

'Give me a moment,' commanded Odo, who spoke

quietly to Thorvald and Arni.

'Arni, you will accompany me. Thorvald, if Arni and I are not back within the hour, bring some of the brethren and make for the hall. Apply caution and ascertain what has happened to us before you come storming in. We have offered peace to these folk. And leave men to take care of the warriors guarding the perimeter.'

'Don't teach your grandmother to suck eggs,' Thorvald replied. 'I know what I am doing.'

'Apologies uncle, you're right. Come Arni.'

'The request was for you alone my lord,' said the horseman.

'Not on this occasion. If your high chief wants my counsel he will see both of us,' stated Odo standing square and unmoving. The horseman hesitated.

'Very well,' he said turning away in the direction of the village.

Odo and Arni followed the horseman on foot towards Drustan's hall. All seemed peaceful as they approached and village life seemed to be continuing as normal. The only change was the number of Cadeyrn's men who stood around in the area outside the hall.

Odo and Arni followed the dismounted messenger inside.

'Ah, Odo, welcome, please sit,' Cadeyrn boomed, 'mead!'

A serving girl brought the clear, heady liquid and placed two full goblets on a table in front of them as they sat on a bench to the side of Cadeyrn and Drustan. Odo and Arni couldn't fail to notice that more of Cadeyrn's men lined the walls and they were fully armed.

'Whatever it is they want it had better be good otherwise we will have hell of a fight on our hands to get out of here,' said Arni in a low growl.

'Relax my friend; I'm sure they want nothing more than a welcoming chat.'

'Welcoming chat my arse,' said Arni.

'And just sip the mead, we need clear heads here.'

Cadeyrn opened the discussion.

'Odo, son of Sigurd, lord of the Skein, and known as Dragon slayer, I have a commission for you. Should you decide to accept, which I strongly recommend you do, you will be handsomely paid and allowed to remain in the encampment you have built alongside my lord Drustan's village.'

Odo, who didn't take kindly to threats, was silent for several moments.

'It depends on the commission,' replied Odo.

'So, you feel you have a choice?' said Cadeyrn.

'I am master of my own destiny lord high chief. No-one owns me or my men and no-one else commands us. We determine where we go and what we do.'

Stillness descended on the hall.

Cadeyrn burst out laughing. 'I admire your confidence my lord Odo. Let me outline the mission I have in mind for you. You are known as Dragon Slayer and it is with dragons in mind that I approach you now.'

'I am listening,' said Odo.

'A terrible being is ravaging the countryside to the west of my territory. It devours our sheep and cattle. It has attacked villagers and borne them off. Ten days ago it tried to carry off my sister. She was unconvinced as to its existence. She is headstrong and was foolish enough to venture into its terrain with a female companion to seek the truth. Thankfully, a couple of my hearth troop had followed her and with the help of a local warrior managed to get her away before the beast could strike. I have sent men to find and kill it but to no avail. The lair of the creature is well hidden and, apart from my sister, no-one has actually seen it in the flesh. You have the reputation as a slayer of dragons and as such I command you to rid my lands of this terror.'

Odo looked hard at Cadeyrn.

'I'm not sure, my lord, you understood what I said to you a moment ago. I am not under anyone's command, least of all yours. Come Arni, we leave this place,' said Odo rising to his feet.

A rasping sound greeted their ears as they stood. The men lining the walls of the hall had drawn their swords and looked at Cadeyrn for a signal.

Unused to being challenged, Cadeyrn kept his anger in check and forced a smile onto his face.

'My lord Odo, an unfortunate turn of phrase, I do you

a disservice. Now please sit and hear me out.'

'I will hear you out,' said Odo, sitting back down with Arni.

The warriors on the walls relaxed, stood back and sheathed their swords.

'I understand from Drustan that you left your lands on a mission to gain glory and a reputation for valour, and that you cannot return until this is so. I also understand that you determined your path lay in ridding lands of dragons, hydras, sea monsters, serpents and mystical beings that terrorise normal folk. I am aware, through Drustan, that you have begun to acquire a reputation as slayer of these kinds of monsters. Is that true?'

'It is my lord.'

'And, in addition to glory gained, you are paid handsomely for your services.'

'It is a perilous path we follow my lord Cadeyrn. I need gold to pay my men, replace equipment and food and carry out repairs to our ship.'

'On completion of your mission I will offer you a chest

of gold and silver,' said Cadeyrn pointing at a small, sturdy wooden chest near his feet.

'It should more than compensate you for your success.'

'I'm sure it will,' replied Odo.

'And as a token of my appreciation I will pay you a tenth in advance.' With that Cadeyrn tossed a leather bag of gold coins at Odo, who deftly caught it in his big hands.

'Do we have deal?'

'I will give you my answer when I have consulted with my men,' replied Odo.

Unused to the democratic ways of the Vikings, Cadeyrn looked bemused.

'Consult with your men? Are you not able to make the decision?'

'In our tradition we discuss major decisions. That is not to say that I, on occasion, do not enforce my will but, in my experience, men who know and readily accept where they are going and what they are fighting for do so with greater commitment than those who do not.'

‘So be it. When can I expect your decision?’ asked Cadeyrn.

‘Later this morning.’

Odo and Arni nodded at Cadeyrn and Drustan, got to their feet and left the village to return to their encampment.

‘Thoughts Arni?’ asked Odo as they walked back.

‘It seems a straight forward assignment and one we are equipped for. I suspect the near death of his sister has prompted this offer. The Regni high chief doesn’t strike me as a generous man or one who cares overmuch for his subjects. We can always use gold and it looks like he will pay us handsomely for this task.’

‘I agree.’

Back at the camp Odo outlined Cadeyrn’s assignment and asked for a vote. The men, who were close to being stir crazy at being cooped up in camp, voted unanimously for the mission.

Odo and Arni returned to the hall to relay their decision with one condition. The decision was greeted with relief and thanks. The condition was that Odo could meet with the high chief's sister to glean what information he could about the beast in question. Caderyn agreed and said he would arrange for her to meet with them near the beast's territory.

The area in question was at least a three day march west from the village through hilly and heavily wooded terrain. The Vikings, who hated walking almost as much as being away from their ship, had insisted to Odo that they should sail as close as possible before proceeding on foot. Odo, who understood that where they were going was close to the coast, agreed.

Chapter Eight

Rumour was rife through the village that the Vikings were to leave the next day to deal with a monster that was ravaging the lands of the Regni to the west.

Siegfried was unhappy but excited. Unhappy that the Vikings were leaving so soon but excited that they were about to embark on a mission of glory. He had arrived at a decision in his mind.

'Easy on that line,' shouted Beigarth, the Vikings shipwright, as the men of Odo's band pulled on ropes that would ease their longship back into the river.

Siegfried had come to say farewell to the Vikings, particularly Arni, and to see what assistance he could render in helping them on their way.

'Siegfried, once we have our craft in the water, you can help load our supplies onto Skidbladnir.'

'What does the name mean?' asked Siegfried who was puffing hard from helping push the craft towards the river bank.

'It means 'blade of wood' and is a magical name. It was the name of the ship used by the beautiful goddess

Freya and was one of the best of longships. Freya is the goddess of beauty, fertility, war, wealth, and magic. All Vikings like Freya.'

Once the ship was settled in the water alongside the settlement's pier, Arni gave orders to some of the men to begin striking camp and to load the equipment on board. Siegfried helped eagerly.

Two hours later all equipment and supplies were stowed on the ship and the Vikings were ready to leave. Drustan with two of his men had come to bid them farewell and to thank them for adhering to the promises they had made.

'Travel well son of Sigurd and may your gods look down on you with favour as you travel west to fulfil your quest.'

'Thank you my Lord Drustan. We have enjoyed our stay here and should you ever have need for our services you only have but to send word. Include this with any message you have and I shall know it is from you and will come with all speed.'

Odo removed a heavily inscribed arm ring from his

left arm and presented it to Drustan who slipped it onto his own arm. They clasped each other's forearms and with a nod Odo stepped away and boarded his ship.

'Why do you look so miserable Arni?' asked Odo.

'It's the boy. He was so keen to help us load our equipment and has now disappeared without saying farewell. I wanted to say goodbye and remind him to keep up his sword practice. He was a good lad and I shall miss his cheerful presence.'

'You know what boys are like. They have the attention span of a newt and no doubt he got distracted and is off doing something else with the other lads of the village.'

'Hmm, maybe,' said Arni scratching his beard reflectively. 'Siegfried didn't strike me as being that kind of boy.'

'Come now, we have work to do,' replied Odo clapping Arni on the back.

Both Arni and Odo assumed their normal positions on the longship, Odo by the steersman and Arni behind the Viking oarsmen from where he called out directions and dictated the speed of rowing.

'Come on lads put your backs into it. You've gone soft with all that easy, village life.'

Despite the fact they had only gone half a mile downstream some of the men were breathing hard. They had lost a certain amount of fitness while ashore. A few days at sea would soon cure that.

The fertile, green land slipped by on either side of the longship as it made its way down river towards the sea. The breeze was light and conditions didn't warrant the hauling up of the large main sail which was stowed in a small cabin at the front of the boat.

Odo could smell the sea and he recognised the chalk bluffs that rose up abruptly from either side of the river. They didn't look nearly as menacing as they had when their ship was being driven hard at them by the ferocious storm of over a month ago. The grass clad chalk cliffs shone a bright green in the sunlight as flocks of gulls swarmed up and over them.

'Lets stand well out to sea and then shadow the coast due west,' said Odo to Agnar his steersman.

'How many days sailing to our destination my lord?' asked Agnar.

'Two, possibly three; it depends on the direction of the winds and their force as you know better than I.'

As he spoke the longship left the waters of the estuary and entered the sea. Almost immediately they felt the wind come veering in from their starboard side. It was a south westerly and sailing against it would be difficult.

'My lord it will be a hard sailing. We should beat south for a day before turning about and returning on a north westerly heading. We will be able to harness the power of the wind in both directions. My sense is this wind will remain from this direction for the next few days,' said Agnar looking up at the sky and sniffing the wind.

Agnar was rarely wrong and Odo agreed with his suggestion.

'Due south it is then, Arni, break out the sail and get it aloft.'

'Arni touched the shoulders of the two Viking

oarsmen nearest him and issued the necessary instructions. Both men shipped their oars and headed towards the bow to retrieve the sail and fasten it to the single main mast.

As the men left their positions Aun, the runemaster, sidled up to Odo.

'We need to make a sacrifice my lord, to keep the gods happy and give us good fortune for the voyage and trials ahead.'

'What do you propose?' asked Odo.

'One of those Celts would have been ideal, but instead we will we offer up this,' said Aun producing a live chicken from under his cloak.

'Do what needs to be done,' said Odo.

At that moment, a piercing yell reached Odo's ears.

'Let me go and stop twisting my arm,' cried a familiar voice.

One of the Vikings who had gone forward to collect the mainsail was pushing a struggling boy towards the rear of the boat and he was proving to be a handful.

'Siegfried! I'd know that voice anywhere,' said Arni.

'The gods have spoken my lord. We have our sacrifice, a Celt. I will make ready.'

'The boy will not be sacrificed,' said Arni addressing Aun.

'That is for our lord Odo to decide. He knows the ways of the gods and that we must make the best sacrifice possible if we are to have a successful voyage.'

'Aun is right,' said Odo.

Arni's face went as black as thunder as he turned to remonstrate with Odo.

'But not on this occasion. Aun go and prepare your chicken. There will be no human blood spilt today.'

Aun gave out a great shriek and began to shout in a tongue no-one understood. He did not look pleased and looked darkly at the struggling form of Siegfried as he was man-handled to the deck in front of Odo and Arni.

'What is the meaning of this Siegfried, your home is back yonder?' asked Odo.

'I want to become a Viking and learn your ways,' cried Siegfried. 'And I knew you wouldn't take me unless I stowed away on board.'

'And what makes you think I won't turn about and return you directly to your village?'

Siegfried looked crestfallen.

'I, I…,' Siegfried stammered, 'I was hoping you would find a use for me and let me stay with you, at least until after this voyage. I can be useful. I know the people, the land and the language when we get to where we are going.'

'Do your father and mother know where you are?'

'I charged my sister with telling them once we had sailed out of sight,' replied Siegfried.

'Hmm, I suspect they will not be happy. I will need to think about this young man. Now go forward to the prow and stay out of everyone's way.'

'Well, that explains why he didn't take his leave of us,' remarked Arni.

'Indeed and don't look so damned pleased,' said Odo.

'It's an omen Odo, a good omen. The boy has been good for us. He warned us of Mochan's treachery and is keen to learn our ways. He has a natural ability and I, for one, would welcome him to our band. And it's true what he says. He is of the Regni and we will still be in Regni territory where we are going and this may be useful.'

Odo gazed out across the sea for several moments.

'We aren't about to turn around and return him, that's for sure. We have a rendezvous with Cadeyrn's sister in three days time and we have an ogre to deal with. The boy stays, but Arni, I'm making you responsible for him, so you had better make sure he stays out of trouble and makes himself useful.'

'That I will,' smiled Arni broadly.

As the crew pulled up the mainsail and the wind began to fill it the rest of the Vikings shipped their oars and relaxed. The longship began to scythe through the swell at a fair clip. Arni made his way forward to where Siegfried sat huddled against the small door of the locker at the prow.

'I hope you know what you are doing,' said Arni.

'I knew as soon as you arrived that my future lay away from the village. I don't fancy being a farmer and I always thought my father wasn't a natural farmer either.'

'Your father was a renowned warrior in Gaul,' said Arni.

'I didn't know that until now,' said Siegfried.

'So, being a warrior may well be in your blood. But you still have a lot to learn,' said Arni.

'Will you teach me?' asked Siegfried.

'There is nothing else to do and of course we will. We need all our men to be capable with spear, shield and sword or axe. And I fancy you will make a skilled swordsman with your natural speed.'

Siegfried grinned.

'In the meantime, observe how we sail the ship and learn what you can by watching. Ask me any questions you like.'

The longship spent the rest of the day forging south. The coast had disappeared from view when towards the end of the afternoon Agnar leant on the steering oar and brought the ship onto a new heading, North West, back towards the coast of Britain. The sail turned on the mast to catch the wind from the south west.

'Beats rowing eh?' said Hakon to Hastein who was

sitting on his bench on the starboard side.

'It sure does,' replied Hastein.

As night fell the temperature dropped rapidly. Fortunately, it was clear and Agnar set his course by the North Star. There would be no land fall this evening for the crew of the longship. They would be sailing through the night.

The men pulled on various fleeces and sheepskins over their leather jerkins to keep warm as Skidbladnir slid through the waters.

As the wind and sea were mild Odo permitted the fire pot to be lit so the men were able to eat a hot stew of beef and vegetables prepared by Bodvar, a short, wide man who acted as the Viking band's cook.

Chapter Nine

The sun was coming up as Siegfried was shaken awake by a young Viking who could not have been much older than him.

'My name is Karl,' said the young man in passable Celtic.

'Mine is Siegfried.'

'I know. Now eat this,' said Karl passing a hard bread roll to Siegfried.

'Arni has asked me to teach you our language and customs. Once you have finished that we will begin.'

Karl was a serious young man and Siegfried wasn't at all sure he would get along with him.

'So, you want to join us; become a Viking?' asked Karl, while Siegfried chewed the bread roll.

'I do. I like adventure and it seems to me you have plenty of adventures.'

'Hah. You know nothing. Every adventure results in hardship or death. Most times both. This is not some children's game we are playing here.'

'I realise that,' said Siegfried.

'Do you? I wonder. Now, let's get to work. I'm going to point out a number of objects on the ship and say them in Norse. You repeat after me.'

An hour later Karl called a halt and suggested they both take a break. Karl left Siegfried at the front of the boat and disappeared back down the craft.

Siegfried was looking out to sea thinking about Karl and the words he had just learnt when he felt his arm seized in a vice like grip.

'Celtic boy, I have need of you,' whispered a voice that belonged to Aun.

'Get away from me!' cried Siegfried.

'Not so loud young pup or I'll cut off one of your ears,' said Aun brandishing a small but vicious looking knife.

'What do you want with me?' asked Siegfried.

'I just want your intestines, liver and kidneys.'

'Over my dead body.'

'That can be arranged,' cackled Aun, 'though a live body is best when the intestines are drawn out. The gods appreciate a live victim.'

Siegfried struggled to get away and was surprised no-one else had noticed his predicament. But the Vikings were gathered in groups chatting, playing games and generally passing the time as their ship proceeded northwards under sail.

Before he could shout out Aun stuffed a gag in his mouth. He then produced a strip of leather hide and bound Siegfried's wrists.

Is this how his adventure would end, thought Siegfried, before it had even begun? Where was Karl? Where was Arni?

Aun tied Siegfried's ankles together and laid him along the deck. He was now out of sight of the nearest group of Vikings and unable to move.

Aun produced a clean white square of linen which he laid on the wooden boards. On this he placed his knife and a large silver bowl. He moved towards Siegfried and lifted Siegfried's shirt revealing his stomach. He picked up what looked like a charcoal crayon and made several marks on Siegfried's skin having first probed the flesh with his fingers.

Siegfried was screaming into his gag but no sound

came out other than a muffled grunt. No-one could hear him.

Aun picked up his curved knife and placed the point against Siegfried's stomach. As he did so he began to chant in an unintelligible tongue. Though he didn't know it this is what saved Siegfried's life.

Arni was amidships when he heard Aun's sacrificial chant. He knew instantly what it was and was surprised as Aun had offered up a chicken the night before. His blood ran cold as realisation struck him. He leapfrogged two Vikings sitting on the deck and plunged along the ship towards the prow.

The first Aun knew of Arni's arrival was when he was hoisted bodily aloft by two powerful arms just as he as about to make his first incision into Siegfried's stomach. He was powerless in Arni's grip.

'Aun, what the hell do you think you are doing? Odo expressly forbade you to carry out any human sacrifices and what do I find here, but you attempting one. I should gut you, throw you overboard and feed you to the fish.'

'Put me down Arni. You will regret interfering with one of the gods chosen ones.'

'You don't scare me little man,' shouted Arni.

'Put him down,' said Odo. 'I will deal with this.'

Arni reluctantly lowered Aun to the deck and let him go.

'Untie the boy Aun,' commanded Odo.

'You don't understand lord. The gods have spoken to me and unless we make a human sacrifice this venture will go ill for us.'

'I don't like going against the gods Aun, but this boy will not be our sacrifice. Do I make myself clear?'

'On your head be it my lord,' acquiesced Aun looking avariciously at Siegfried.

'Now untie him, immediately!'

Aun released Siegfried from his bindings who moved quickly behind Arni.

'Don't worry lad, I won't let this weasel touch you again. You'd better come to the stern with me where I can keep an eye on you.'

Odo, Arni and Siegfried made their way back down

the longship to the stern.

'Land dead ahead!' cried the Viking watch, as the grey outline of the southern coast of Britain came into view.

'Let's hope we have judged our navigation well,' said Odo to Agnar. 'We need a river called Arun to take us to the dragon's lair.

It took the rest of the day for the Viking's ship to close on the coast. By early evening they could make out the opening of an inlet.

'Find us a beach where we can hove to for the night,' said Odo to Agnar.

As the longship neared the coast Agnar spotted the ideal refuge to the east of the inlet. It was shingle beach that stretched away in either direction, and it was easy work to drive their ship ashore and secure it in the shallows.

As the craft touched the beach a party of Vikings under Thorvald's direction leapt ashore to secure the immediate area and assess any danger. Apart from some goats there was no evidence of any humans, though the goatherd could not be far away.

The Vikings set up camp on the beach. In no time a fire was blazing and Bodvar was cooking a stew of goat mixed with vegetables brought from Siegfried's village. It smelt wonderful and the nearest Vikings were looking on hungrily.

A barrel of mead was broached and the Vikings gathered around the fire to eat and quaff horns of mead. The mood was relaxed as Odo asked Skorri, the band's bard, to entertain them with a Saga, a tale about Viking voyages, battles that took place and famous warriors. Skorri needed no prompting as his rich voice began to tell a story about a famous ancestor of Odo's.

Siegfried sat cross-legged by the fire unable to understand much as his Norse was rudimentary. But he enjoyed the camaraderie of these fierce men and their free attitude to life. This was better than being bound to a village and fetching and carrying all day when he wasn't being trained how to farm.

As he looked up he saw Aun was watching him from across the fire and he shivered. That was one man he had to stay away from. As he gazed at Aun he saw him drag a finger across his throat while pointing at him with his other hand. This was not good. He'd better make sure he was close by Arni when he slept this night.

Unfortunately, sleep was going to be delayed as Odo issued instructions for Karl and Siegfried to take the first watch of the night; two hours up on the bluffs above the beach.

'He's but a boy,' said Arni to Odo. 'We can't rely on him.'

'If he is going to become a Viking he has to learn and what better place than on a beach that is in Regni territory. Karl will keep an eye on him. Besides, with Caderyn's protection, I don't anticipate any trouble.'

On that Odo could not be more wrong.

It was nearly two hours later when Karl hissed a warning to Siegfried.

'Quiet. We have company, men with swords to our left.'

Siegfried, who had excellent night vision, could make out a group of men moving silently towards the edge of the bluffs above the beach.

‘Regni,’ he whispered to Karl.

‘We need to forewarn the camp,’ said Karl. ‘But we cannot, without letting them know we are here.’

Before Karl could do anything else, Siegfried stood up and walked nonchalantly towards the men calling out.

‘Hail men of the Regni. What business brings you here?’

Delivered in the Regni dialect of the Celtic tongue the men were caught by surprise.

‘I am Morcant, chief of the Angenmaer of the Regni,’ came a voice. ‘And who are you?’

‘I am Siegfried of the Leonids of the Regni and I come on our high lord Cadeyrn’s business.’

‘You are but a boy,’ came the contemptuous reply. ‘What do you know of Cadeyrn?’

Siegfried accurately described him and told him about the mission of the men on the beach. He omitted to tell them they were Vikings and not of their race. The chief of the Angenmaer was impressed.

‘I have yet to hear about this quest but what you say about Cadeyrn is true. His sister was in grave danger and it was one of my men who helped Cadeyrn's hearth warriors save the lady. I will leave you in peace tonight but when you come upriver tomorrow, we will meet again. I need to brief your leader. What is his name?'

'Odo, my lord.'

Not a Regni name,' replied Morcant.

'No, my lord,' said Siegfried lapsing into silence.

The chief of the Angenmaer looked at Siegfried for several moments.

'We will meet again tomorrow when you arrive at the barrow by the ford. You will not to able to navigate beyond that point?'

'Very good my lord,' said Siegfried.

With that, Morcant and his warriors retraced their steps inland and left Siegfried and Karl, who hadn't spoken a word, alone.

'That took some balls,' said Karl.

'Not really. They are my people after all.'

Nevertheless, that was brave thing to do. What did you agree with their chief?'

Siegfried recounted what had taken place as two

Vikings appeared on the bluffs to relieve them of their watch.

Karl told them briefly what had happened and not to expect any further visits that night.

'We had better make a report to Odo,' said Karl.

'Well done Siegfried,' said Odo. 'They will be surprised to encounter us tomorrow. Now get some sleep. You've earned it.'

Siegfried sought out Arni's bulk by the fire and settled down next to him. If Aun was going to come for him in the early hours of the morning he wanted to be within touching distance of Arni. With that secure thought he fell instantly asleep.

Chapter Ten

The following morning the men breakfasted on the remnants of the cold stew and hard bread. As the sun rose in the sky they eased their longship down the beach and into the water. The inlet they were looking for was but half a mile away. With its opening protected from the westerly winds by a coastline that jutted out due south on the western side of the estuary, this was the entrance to the River Arun.

'Oars out men, let's be having you,' shouted Arni.

The Vikings slipped their oars through the holes in the side of the longship and began to row the sleek craft towards the inlet. It was a calm day with the sun shining down from a blue sky. Gulls circled overhead as they looked, hopefully, for any scraps of food.

'Easy,' said Arni, as Agnar steered the longship into the mouth of the river and the men began to pull upstream against the current.

Eventually the river began to shallow and Siegfried pointed out a huge mound of earth on the left bank of the river.

‘The barrow by the ford, my lord.’

‘What is the barrow?’ asked Odo.

‘It is an ancient burial mound that houses the bodies of people who were here long before us.’

‘Agnar, we need to moor against the eastern bank of the river,’ said Odo.

‘Yes, my lord.’

Agnar guided the longship expertly through the shallows until it came to rest against the eastern bank.

Two of the men jumped ashore to secure the ship at either end against the riverside.

It was Thorvald who first sensed the danger as reflected sunlight off metal caught his eye.

‘Men to the east my lord,’ he said to Odo.

Odo followed his outstretched hand and saw a solid phalanx of Regni warriors calmly watching their arrival. Their calmness helped to quell the anxiety Odo felt in his guts.

‘Brothers, pick up your swords and shields and form a shield wall on the shore, two lines, one behind the other,’ commanded Odo. ‘I want it done quietly, as if we were on a training exercise. Siegfried, get yourself in front alongside me.'

The Vikings gathered their gear and stepped ashore in a collected and composed fashion. None of them wore their mail shirts, as the day was warm and trouble was not expected, but armed with shield and sword they still presented a formidable sight.

A man on a chestnut coloured horse edged away from his comrades towards the Vikings, accompanied by two others.

When he was within twenty yards, he hailed them.

'I saw you encamped on the beach last night and thought you men of the Regni sent by Cadeyrn to rid our land of the terrible monster that lurks nearby here. But I see that you are nothing of the kind and must wonder what business you have here.'

Odo pushed Siegfried forward and indicated he should speak.

'My lord Morcant, may I introduce my lord Odo. He has been commissioned by our high chief the lord Cadeyrn to rid our land of the monster.'

'I know nothing of this,' said Morcant. 'Cadeyrn has sent me no word.'

'What I say is true,' said Siegfried.

The horseman to Morcant's left spoke.

'He is but a boy my lord, no doubt a captive slave of these barbarians. Why should we believe what he says? No doubt they have put him up to this. I can't see any other reason why a boy of the Regni would be with these marauders.'

'I'm telling you the truth,' shouted Siegfried.

'I agree with Oswald,' said the other man. 'The boy sounds desperate and hysterical. No doubt these barbarians have a hold over him and he would say anything.'

Morcant, an impetuous man, looked at Siegfried and Odo and made up his mind.

'You will depart this shore immediately and head back out to sea. If you do so, we will let you go without hindrance. If you choose to stay your ground, we will cut you down.'

Odo looked directly at Morcant.

'We have an agreement with your high chief Cadeyrn to rid your land of this monster and that is what we intend to do. We stay and will see out our mission.'

Morcant looked challengingly at Odo for several moments before wheeling his horse away back to his line of warriors.

Minutes later Morcant's men began to chant and bang their weapons against their shields. A large man led the chanting and began to work the Celtic warriors into a frenzy. They appeared in no hurry to attack the Viking force.

'We have a few moments Arni,' said Odo. 'Get as many men as possible into their chain mail. This could be a bloody business.'

Half of the Viking band slipped back on board the longship and donned their mail brynjas and iron helmets. The wealth they had gained from their various missions meant they could afford armour and weaponry that was superior to that normally worn by the tribal warriors they had encountered in Gaul and Britain. This was a powerful edge in any combat they were involved in. All the men had swords though several preferred the axe. Every member of the band had a shield made of fir or poplar wood bound with iron making them less susceptible to splitting from an opponent's blow, and all the men had at least three, well made, ash spears. A spear was the primary weapon of Odin, the king of the Norse gods, and no self-respecting Viking would be without at least one.

By contrast, Morcant's men were mainly covered in leather; few wore helmets and they bore an assortment of weapons - cudgels, spears, swords and axes.

By the time the Vikings in mail and helmets had reassembled on the banks of the river the men of the Regni had begun to advance on them hurling insults and abuse.

Odo's men remained silent, watching, professionally, the advance of their opponents.

Arni looked at Odo. 'Shall we cast a volley of spears?'

'No, we will not be the first to shed blood here. No spears. We will rely on the strength of our shield wall and use our swords and axes if we have to.'

When the two lines of warriors were ten yards apart the Regni halted for a moment and went silent. Their leader shouted something unintelligible and at his signal they surged forward and charged into the Viking shield wall. Odo's men met their advance with a grunt as their interlocked shields slowed down the assault.

While those in the front row concentrated on keeping their shields locked and solid, those in the second row thrust their spears, swords and axes at any part of their opponents they could reach. Without armour the men of the Regni suffered horribly as the Viking weapons hacked at heads, arms, shoulders and legs. Many of the Regni fell and reeled backwards impeding those who supported them from behind.

As the injury count rose, Morcant made a sign and his standard bearer lifted a horn to his mouth and sounded the retreat. Morcant's men broke away. The Vikings were keen to follow and bring an end to the battle but at a shout from Arni they remained where they were. Apart from superior weaponry they had superior discipline.

Morcant's men re-formed and his reserve moved

forward to join the next charge. These were his own household warriors and would prove a tougher proposition for the Vikings than the men they had faced in the first wave of the attack.

Apart from a few cuts and bruises the Vikings were in good shape and readied themselves for the next attack.

As Morcant was about to signal his men forward, a squadron of heavily armed horsemen on huge chargers appeared from the trees to his right and bore down on the scene of battle. Morcant recognised the banner of the hearth troop of his high chief Cadeyrn and raised his hand to stop the advance of his warriors.

'About time,' said Arni. 'We could do without this unnecessary trouble.'

The horses pulled up in front of Morcant and a man on a white charge began to berate him in no uncertain fashion.

'I wouldn't want to be in Morcant's shoes,' said Arni to Odo.

The argument between the warrior on the white horse and Morcant went on for some time but the end result was that Morcant and his forces withdrew inland back towards their fortified settlement leaving the troop of heavily armed warriors on their own. The man on the white horse dismounted and approached Odo and his men.

'I must apologise for that reception my lord Odo. I am Badeyrn, half-brother to Cadeyrn, a prince of the Regni and captain of his household warriors.'

'Welcome my lord Badeyrn. You arrived not a moment too soon.'

'Aye, that I could see. Morcant has a temper and is a rash man but he is brave and loyal to our high chief.'

'No doubt, but his rashness could have got him and his men killed.'

'He understands that and will make amends at a feast tonight in his hall. You and your men will be welcome. We need to discuss your mission and you need to meet our lady Nevena, sister to Cadeyrn and myself.

**

It was early evening when Odo and his men set off for the walk to the hall. The only weaponry they carried were their knives but four men were left behind to guard the longship and four more, fully armed, set off for the village bearing as many swords as they could carry.

One of Odo's men had scouted out the village during the afternoon and had found a large, densely wooded copse close by the chief's hall where the four armed men could hide out and keep a watch on the evening's proceedings as they unfolded. Should there be any treachery they would fight their way into the hall and distribute the swords. Odo thought any trouble was unlikely but he wanted to be prepared.

Siegfried and Karl made up two of the four who were to be left behind to guard the longship. Hastein and Hakon were the other two.

'Why is it that I always seem to draw the short straw Hastein?' asked Hakon. 'Here we are in the cool of the evening with no mead, no fat haunches of meat to get our teeth into, no roaring fire and no wenches to make eyes at.'

'Agh, who wants to be in a stuffy hall having to make small talk with the Celts? I know I don't. Give me the fresh air and the peace of this riverside any time.'

'It's all right for you,' complained Hakon. 'You don't drink and you don't eat much either.

Hastein, who was a thin and wiry man, couldn't disagree.

'We have the remains of Bodvar's stew which we can reheat,' said Siegfried.

'Aye lad, that we do. In fact why don't you and Karl do just that. We might as well enjoy ourselves while we can. And I'll see if we have some mead stashed away.'

'The boys should not be partaking of the mead,' said Hastein emphatically. 'It will do them no good and they have to be sharp if they are keeping watch with us.'

'Okay, okay, I'll drink on my own,' grumbled Hakon.

'It won't do you any good either. You need to be sharp tonight, especially as we have the two boys on watch with us; no disrespect to you two,' said Hastein nodding at Karl and Siegfried.

'Why are you always so sensible?' said Hakon as he put a stopper back into the leather bag of mead and returned it to where he found it.

Siegfried and Karl soon had a vigorous fire going and the stew bubbling away. It was warm by the fire and the four Vikings were quite content though they knew that soon two of them would have to leave the fire to keep guard. It promised to be a long night keeping watch.

**

In the hall, Odo and his men were about to take their seats. Under the gaze of Badeyrn, a powerfully built, authoritative figure, Morcant was welcoming to the point of obsequiousness.

'I must apologise for our reaction today my lord Odo, but in my position I'm sure you would have behaved in much the same way.'

Odo was not sure he would have done but he nodded all the same without saying anything.

His mind was focussed elsewhere and the object of this attention was standing between Morcant and Badeyrn. The lady Nevena was a tall, statuesque woman with a mane of auburn hair held back by a circlet of gold studded with precious stones. Her eyes were green in colour and she had a generous smile. Odo, who had little experience of high born women and, in fact, women in general, was smitten. Her beauty left him feeling uncomfortable.

Unbeknownst to him, the lady Nevena felt much the same way. She had never met such a big man, or one with such fair coloured hair. It was rare to meet a man who was taller than her and Odo was taller by many inches. A well educated woman, to her he looked like one of the Greek heroes she had heard and read about.

'My lord Odo, may I introduce my sister the lady Nevena,' said Badeyrn.

'Welcome my lord Odo,' said Nevena. 'I understand from my brother that you have a reputation for dragon slaying and that you will rid our land of the monster that almost did for me and my hand maiden.'

'I will do my best, my lady, to accomplish this task.'

'If there is anything I can do to help then you have but to ask.'

'I would like to get a description from you of the monster and where you last saw it before you were rescued,' said Odo.

'Of course,' replied Nevena.

'But not tonight,' interrupted Badeyrn. 'Tonight, we welcome you and your men to the lands of the Angenmaer of the Regni. We shall relax, eat, drink and hear songs from our bard. There will be plenty of time tomorrow to hatch our plans and for you to question the lady Nevena about the monster.'

'As you wish my lord,' replied Nevena, smiling at Odo.

Food and mead were served and soon Vikings and Regni were enjoying a spirited conversation and, to all intents and purposes, behaving like old friends. The short battle on the banks of the river Arun, which had resulted in several of the Regni being badly injured, seemed forgotten.

It was in the early hours of the morning when Siegfried, who was on watch, observed the unsteady progress of the mass of Vikings back towards the ship. Fortunately, it was a mild night and the Vikings bedded down where they could, wrapping their cloaks around them. Some found space on the deck of the longship, others on the river bank. For Siegfried, Karl, Hakon and

Hastein, the night was not over. Their watch would continue until daybreak, two hours on, two hours off.

Chapter Eleven

The sun was well up when the majority of the Vikings awoke. Odo was already up and in conversation with Arni and Thorvald.

Siegfried and Karl had just completed their last watch and were planning to grab some sleep on board the longship. Arni noticed them boarding the vessel.

'How was the night's watch?' asked Arni.

'Uneventful,' replied Siegfried.

'Good,' replied Arni. 'That's the best outcome. Now get some sleep.'

Siegfried rolled himself in a blanket, pulled the hood of his cloak over his face and fell instantly asleep. Karl did likewise.

Meanwhile, Odo, who had stripped off his clothing, jumped into the river for a wash and to clear his head. The cold water certainly sharpened his senses and made his skin glow. When he came ashore he towelled himself down and rummaged in his chest for his best clothing. Arni could not fail but to notice.

'And who are we trying to impress today?' asked Arni.

'Surely not that little toad Morcant and not Badeyrn either?'

'You know full well,' replied Odo.

'Ah, so the lady Nevena has cast her spell over you has she?'

'I don't deny that I am taken with her but if we are going to catch and slay this monster we need her assistance.'

'I'm sure we do. But do you need to dress in your finery to enlist her help?'

Odo looked embarrassed. 'It can do nothing but aid our venture,' he replied lamely.

Arni burst out laughing. 'I better look out my finest gear as well then.'

Once Odo was clad in his mail shirt, gleaming in the early morning sun, he slipped the leather strapping over his shoulder that held his sword, Dragon Slayer, in its scabbard by his side and fastened his bright blue cloak around his shoulders. With his many gold arm rings glistening on his muscular arms he was the embodiment of Odin, the Allfather, god of war and death.

With Arni and Thorvald standing alongside, equally dressed in their finest mail and clothing, they made a powerful impression on the horsemen who approached with the lady Nevena in their midst.

The sight of Odo took Nevena's breath away. Though her brothers, Cadeyrn and Badeyrn, were commanding and impressive in their own right, neither had the height or presence of Odo, nor the surprising beauty.

The leader of the group of horsemen came to a halt and they all dismounted. The lady Nevena, who was wearing breeches, a leather jerkin and a cloak did not look out of place among the men. Giving her bridle to one of the men she walked towards Odo.

'Good morning my lord, I trust you slept well.'

'I slept extremely well my lady,' said Odo exaggerating, as he still nursed a heavy head from the mead and rich food he had consumed the night before.

'Walk with me a while,' she commanded.

Odo removed his helmet, handed it to Arni, who winked, and set off along the river bank with Nevena. After some minutes they came to a fallen oak tree.

'Please sit,' asked Nevena. 'Now, what would you like to know about the monster?'

'I'd like to know what it looks like, and where and when you last saw it.'

The lady Nevena answered his questions as fully as her memory allowed.

'Now that we have that out of the way, tell me a little more about yourself and where you are from.'

'My father is Sigurd, lord of the Skein, a people who hail from a land called Norway far across the sea, north east from here. We are called Vikings and we left our homeland to seek glory, valour and riches.'

'I understand that, but what caused you to leave?'

'That is a long story my lady but essentially I was banished.'

Odo went onto describe what had happened and why he had left his mother country.

Tears glistened in Nevena's eyes at the seeming injustice.

'You poor man, was there no other choice?'

'No, my lady.'

'So, you are now here to defeat yet another monster.'

'I am my lady and we will. With what you have told me today we will be prepared and we will prevail.'

The lady Nevena stood up and Odo followed. She came towards him and taking his head in both hands she reached up and kissed him on the cheek.

'I wish you luck my lord.'

'We will need all the luck we can get my lady and thank you for wishing us well.'

Odo, whose head was in a spin, accompanied the lady Nevena back along the river bank towards the Regni horse warriors whose captain was waiting impatiently.

'Are we done here my lady?' asked the captain of horse.

'We are done when I say so,' Nevena replied. And with that she turned to Odo.

'I would be interested in seeing your ship my lord.'

'Of course my lady,' replied Odo, taken off balance.

Odo helped Nevena on board the longship and gave her a guided tour.

'I think we had better finish now. The captain of horse

looks distinctly unimpressed,' said Nevena, finding Odo's hand with her own and squeezing it hard. She flashed him a dazzling smile.

With that Odo and Nevena disembarked.

'Captain, I'm ready to leave,' said Nevena, mounting her horse in one easy, unassisted, bound.'

With that, the troop of horse set off back towards Morcant's settlement. When they were fifty yards away the captain of the troop turned around and cantered back to Odo.

'With respect my lord, I would be careful about how you pursue any friendship with the lady Nevena. My lord Cadeyrn would not be amused.' With that he pulled his horse round and rejoined his mounted warriors.

'Good job,' said Arni. 'You've made an enemy of him and like as not Cadeyrn and Badeyrn when they get to hear of this.

'But nothing happened,' protested Odo. 'And we needed her intelligence.'

'It would be obvious to a blind man the electricity that passed between you. Though, I do say she took the initiative.'

'It's all academic anyway, said Odo wistfully. 'I doubt we will see her again.'

'So, what did you learn?'

'Enough to give us a clue as to where we might find this monster that has eluded all the best scouts that Cadeyrn could throw at the problem.'

**

A little after mid-day a rider appeared at the fringe of the camp the Vikings had set up on the bank of the river. He cantered up to the man on watch and introduced himself.

'I am Seisal. I come from the high chief Cadeyrn.
Please take me to your leader.'

The man was led towards Odo, where he repeated his introduction.

'Welcome Seisal, we have been expecting you. And why have you been selected for this quest?'

'I am the lord Cadeyrn's most experienced scout and have recently returned from the dun of the lord high chief of the Atrebates, who are our cousins.'

'I'm sure we shall need all the help we can get. Come and sit with me and let us plan our approach to locating and killing this monster.'

Odo, and his inner circle of Arni, Thorvald and Ingvar, sat on recently cut roundels of oak. Seisal joined them. Bodvar brought mead. After the men had toasted each other Odo got down to business.

'What do we know about this dragon?' asked Odo. 'Seisal, tell us what you know?'

'Yes my lord. The monster appears suddenly, without warning, and targets sheep and cattle which it kills and drags off. It also attacks any villagers who may get in its way or be nearby. It seems to have a preference for womenfolk. From those who have seen it and lived and the lady Nevena is the only one I know of who has survived to tell the tale, it appears to be some twenty feet long, of a dull red and greenish colour with wings. The skin is leathery in appearance and its head is small though it has a long snout. It spews venom which is purple in colour. When this venom strikes its prey, it turns it into a liquefied mass which, I believe, makes for easier consumption.'

'Very nasty,' said Thorvald. 'Do you have any idea where this beast's lair is to be located?'

'No, my lord, on that we are completely at a loss.'

'Are there any caves around here?' asked Ingvar.

'No, the land around here is largely flat.'

'The monster must have a well hidden lair given its size. How can it vanish so easily and not be seen until it next appears to devour an animal or some poor unfortunate being?' said Arni.

'That has been the subject of much discussion at the lord Cadeyrn's council.'

'Does it appear at any particular time of day?' asked Thorvald.

'It seems to appear at dusk, only, which aids its disappearance. By the time our villagers have realised it has carried off their cattle it's too dark to track the beast. And come the following morning there is no trace.'

'How large is its territory? Does it roam far?' inquired Thorvald.

'It appears to contain its activities to within our tribal lands and near Morcant's settlement, just east of here.'

Odo, who had remained silent until this point, now spoke up.

'What I know is that the beast is dripping with water when it appears and attacks cattle or men and women. Are you aware of this Seisal?'

'No my lord, no-one has mentioned that to me.'

'What do you think that tells us?' asked Odo, addressing the men who sat around him.

'It lives in the river!' said Arni.

'A good suggestion Arni, but the river here is shallow and is not deep enough to hide a monster of the size we know it to be.'

'Are there other bodies of water around here Seisal, lakes or big ponds?' asked Thorvald.

'There are many,' said Seisal. 'We are on a on a coastal flood plain here and there is a lot of water.'

'My theory is that it lives within a deep pond or large pool of water. How many such pools or ponds of water are there in the vicinity Seisal?' asked Odo.

‘At least six or seven,’ he replied.

‘Tomorrow we will scout out these ponds,’ said Odo.

Chapter Twelve

Following a breakfast of pork and bread, Odo made ready to set off with a handful of his men. Among them were Arni, Asbjorn, Finn, Geir, Ingvar, Rolf, Karl and Siegfried. Thorvald was left in charge of the rest of the men and the ship.

'You travel with few men and a couple of boys,' said Thorvald as he bade his farewell.

'I don't anticipate any trouble,' replied Odo. 'We should be safe among the Regni. Skidbladnir is our most important asset so guard it well.'

'As you said my lord, I don't anticipate any trouble,' smiled Thorvald.

The band of men then set out with Seisal as their guide.

During the next two days they explored seven ponds and small lakes. At first appearance they all looked promising but most were shallow and could not have contained the ogre they were looking for.

They narrowed their search to two. Both appeared deep; deeper than a man could wade across without touching the bottom.

'If the monster is truly from this area then these are the two ponds we need to explore thoroughly,' said Odo.

The first of the ponds was located in a grove of trees and soft ground.

'I need a volunteer, someone who can swim well under water and is not afraid to dive deep and explore the floor of this pond. Who is the best swimmer among us?' asked Odo.

The men all looked at each other, for though they were all brave men, none fancied ducking down deep under the placid looking water. They all feared the goddess Ran and her net, set to catch the unwary who ventured into waters unknown, for even though this wasn't the sea, her usual habitat, there was no way of knowing that she wouldn't inhabit an inshore water like this small lake.

'I am an excellent swimmer,' said Siegfried who began stripping off his clothing.

'Siegfried this is not of your concern,' said Odo.

'Don't worry my lord. Among the Leonids I am always

the one who can stay under water the longest,' replied Siegfried.

'Nevertheless, I do not wish you to undertake this exploration.'

'Come on brother, what are you afraid of?' jeered Ingvar. 'The boy says he can do it. Let him show his worth. It's about time he did considering he's an extra mouth to feed and hasn't proved his worth as a warrior.'

Odo glared at his half-brother Ingvar who stood smiling at him. Arni fidgeted in the background uncomfortable with the way things were going. Odo reached a decision.

'All right Siegfried, show us what you can do. But at the first sign of danger I want you back out of the water as quickly as you can.'

'Yes my lord.'

Siegfried stripped off his clothes, took a deep breath and dived gracefully into the pond.

Two minutes went by, then a third.

'This was not a good idea,' muttered Arni concerned.

'The boy says he can swim. Let him prove it,' said

Ingvar enjoying Arni's discomfort.

Another minute went by and just as Odo was beginning to think he would have to go in after him Siegfried's head broke the surface of the water. Breathing hard he swam easily to the side of the small lake.

'It's deep my lord, too deep for me to reach the bottom and I went at least thirty feet down. I will have another go.'

'No, Siegfried I'm sure what you say is true. There is no need for another attempt.'

But Siegfried took no notice. He swam out into the middle of the body of the water, took another deep breath and duck dived out of sight. The waters were clear and the men could easily follow his form as he angled down straight and deep. As the men watched he disappeared from view. This time it felt as if at least five minutes had gone by before they saw his figure coming straight back up.

Siegfried burst out of the water and pulled for the bank.

'It's no good my lord, I couldn't reach the bottom. It's clear a long way down but it then gets dark and I couldn't see or touch the bottom.'

'Right, that's enough Siegfried. Out of the water with you and get dried and dressed,' commanded Odo.

It was close to evening so Odo ordered the men to set up camp just below a ridge above the pond. Soon they had a fire roaring away and several fat pigeons roasting above the flames. With their ever present mead and some fresh bread brought by the owner of the land on where the pond lay, the men gathered round the fire in good spirits looking forward to their meal.

Odo beckoned Seisal over to come and sit by him.

'Are you sure the ponds we have looked at in the last two days are the only waters within which the monster could dwell?'

'Yes, my lord. The monster has never been seen outside an area that encompasses half a day's ride from my lord Morcant's hall.'

Odo sat back and thought hard. He appeared to have gone into a half sleep before he suddenly sat up and grabbed Seisal by the arm.

'I have it. Does the ogre appear in winter as well as summer?' asked Odo.

'The seasons make no difference as to when it appears my lord. It has been known to strike in the depths of winter when the land is as hard as iron from the frost and snow.'

'When even the lakes and ponds freeze over?'

'Indeed, my lord. Nothing escapes the great father, god of winter, harvest, the sky, animals and mountains. When the cold comes everything freezes over.'

'Is there a pond or lake that doesn't freeze over?'

'Not that I know of my lord.'

Odo was not so easily put off.

'Tell me Sesial, have you seen this pond frozen in winter?'

'I have my lord.'

What about the other pond near Lymineir?'

'That, I cannot answer my lord.'

'Right,' said Odo triumphantly. 'Tomorrow we decamp there.'

**

The following morning the men set off in high spirits. They were well rested and well fed, though one or two nursed heavy heads from the excellent mead.

As they approached the pond near Lymineir, Seisal began to look nervous. Odo picked up on it immediately.

'You look worried Seisal,' said Odo.

'I am my lord. This pond we visit is on holy ground. Lymineir is the sanctuary of druids and I fear we may not be allowed access.'

'If your high lord Cadeyrn wishes his lands rid of this monster then they will surely allow us access.'

'The druids are not answerable to normal men, my lord; no matter how high born. They only answer to the high priestess who resides on the isle of Mona which is far from here.'

'I'm not deterred so easily Seisal. Let's see what they have to say once we get there.'

How they knew Odo and his men were coming was a mystery but as they crested a rise, near the holy land of Lymineir, several men in white robes were arranged in a line across their path. The most senior appeared to be an old man with a long flowing white beard. He raised his arm as they approached calling the band to a halt. Odo and Sesial walked ahead to greet the old man.

'Seisal, tell him about our mission and that we come on the high lord Cadeyrn's orders.'

Sesial did as he was instructed. A heated exchange of words followed.

'It's no good my lord. He says we are not welcome here and that the lord Cadeyrn has no jurisdiction over their land.'

Most of the Vikings who could understand Celtic had followed the discussion. Ingvar was the first to speak.

'Are we going to be put off by this old goat? I say that unless he lets us pass we string him and his brethren up and get on with what we have been paid to do.'

Rolf, who was ever present at Ingvar's side, nodded vigorously in agreement.

'Very helpful brother, we need tact not brute force in this situation. These people are not our enemies.

'Hah!' spat Ingvar.

'Seisal, tell white beard that we wish him no harm and that we will send word to the high lord Cadeyrn for his guidance and that in the meantime we will camp over yonder by the stream there.'

Seisal relayed Odo's words. The old man grunted and spoke again for almost a minute before turning away with his followers towards an open gate set in a wooden stockade that surrounded their dwelling. Once inside they closed the gate leaving Odo and his men on the path where they had met.

'Let's storm the stockade and ransack this excuse of a fortified settlement and get on with what we are here for. They may even have some gold, though no women I fear,' suggested Ingvar.

'Ingvar, hold your tongue,' commanded Odo exasperated. 'We will send word to Cadeyrn and negotiate our way around this problem. In the meantime we need fresh meat. We could be here for some days. Take Rolf and see what you can find among the woods on the other side of the stream.'

Rolf was good with the bow, one of only a handful of

Vikings who could use the weapon proficiently. Ingvar looked at Odo insolently for several seconds before turning away and beckoning Rolf to follow him.

'I don't know why you brought him,' said Arni. 'He's nothing but trouble.'

'That's exactly why I brought him. I need him to keep an eye on him at all times. Who knows what mischief he might have got up to back with Thorvald?'

Odo despatched Seisal for Cadeyrn's hall.

'Tell him we need access to the land of the Lymineir Druids and that if he can come in person that this would be much appreciated. If not in person, then he must send someone who the druids will listen to.'

'I understand my lord.'

With that Seisal departed just as Ingvar and Rolf emerged from the nearby woodland with a young deer over their shoulders.

'Well done brother, we shall eat well tonight,' said Odo.

Invar smiled for, though he didn't always agree with Odo, he appreciated his praise.

Chapter Thirteen

Asbjorn, who was on watch, felt it first; a rhythmic beating on the ground which signified heavy horses. He was on a small rise by an oak tree some way from where Odo and his men had set up camp; He stood up for a better look.

A small troop of six horses were cantering easily towards him across open ground. He relaxed as he recognised Seisal on the lead horse. He trotted back towards the Viking camp.

'We have company my lord,' he said to Odo who was busy sketching a diagram in the earth at his feet with a stick, closely watched by Arni.

'Ah, that was fast work by Seisal. Now we may get somewhere,' said Odo.

The horsemen drew nearer. If he was expecting to see the high lord Cadeyrn, Odo was disappointed. In his place rode the lady Nevena. Odo was surprised.

As the horsemen came to a halt on the outskirts of the Viking camp, Odo went forward to help the lady Nevena off her horse.

'Thank you for your offer of assistance my lord, but I do not need it,' she said as she athletically jumped down from her mount.

'You look disappointed to see me.'

'On the contrary my lady, just puzzled, I was expecting the high lord Cadeyrn.'

'He has no jurisdiction here, whereas I do,' she said mysteriously, as she walked towards the centre of the Viking camp.

'Now, some breakfast and a drink would be much appreciated. I have ridden without to get here as fast I could today,' she said.

'Of course my lady; Siegfried fetch the lady food and drink,' commanded Odo. It was Siegfried's turn to serve breakfast for the men.

'Now, perhaps you would be good enough to tell me why you have come,' asked Odo.

'Are you not pleased to see me?' replied the lady Nevena, her eyes flashing.

'I would always be pleased to see you but we have a dragon to slay and need access to the druids' enclosure.

This is not the time for social pleasantries.'

'Ah, I see,' said Nevena. 'Let me enlighten you. I can gain you access to the druids' land.'

'You can, how?' said Odo disbelievingly.

'I am a druid priestess. I studied under the high priestess of Mona, in the sacred birthplace of druidism. These men here will listen to me.'

'You surprise me,' said Odo. 'I had no idea you were a holy person, a dreamer, a diviner of the gods wishes.'

'I'm not that holy Odo. Politically, it pays for me to be a member of the Druid class. Next to the leaders of the Celtic tribes they are the most powerful members of our society, some would argue the most powerful, and I believe in their powers. They can heal, foresee what is to come, set the laws which we live by and are among the wisest of our men and womenfolk. They are not to be underestimated. They can perform powerful magic. I have seen it done.'

'No doubt,' said Odo. 'If you can get us into their enclosure and to the pond, therein, then I will be grateful.'

‘That will be no problem. Now come with me,’ said Nevena rising to her feet.

The lady Nevena approached the druid stockade accompanied by two of her men and Odo and Arni. She called out when she was within twenty yards.

The same men who had stood up to Odo and his men the day before appeared. The oldest, white beard knelt down before her and uttered a string of words in fast Celtic which Odo and Arni could not understand.

Nevena was calm, sympathetic and spoke like a mother to a child. Eventually the old man got to his feet and, after some discussion, turned away and gestured for the gates of the stockade to be opened.

Nevena turned towards Odo and Arni.

‘He’s not entirely happy and says the dragon does not reside in his pond but he will let you and your men in to conduct an investigation.’

‘Thank the gods,’ said Arni.

Odo asked Arni, Finn, Geir and Siegfried and the Lady Nevena to accompany him into the druids’ enclosure.

‘You have to leave your weapons here. The druids won’t countenance armed men within their settlement,’ said Nevena.

‘We can’t do that,’ replied Odo. ‘There is an ogre within their pond and we need to be armed should we disturb it and it attacks us.’

Nevena looked at Odo. ‘Then you had better give me few more minutes to discuss this with them.’ With that the lady Nevena took the old druid aside. After a lengthy discussion Nevena returned to Odo.

‘He has agreed but your weapons need to be given into my keeping while you conduct your explorations.’

Odo was not happy about this but agreed reluctantly.

The pond in question lay beyond the stockade. It was small, about thirty feet across and set within a heavy grove of trees and undergrowth. It was covered by a rich looking layer of green algae and leaves that had fallen from the trees. A strange smell emanated from it. The pond would be easy to miss if one did not know it was there.

‘This does not look promising,’ said Arni. ‘It stinks and

nothing appears to have come by here for some time.'

If Odo was disappointed he didn't show it.

'My lady, can you please ask the old man if this pond freezes in winter?'

'Why are you so concerned with whether a pond freezes or not?' asked Arni.

'The dragon appears in winter, no?'

'Yes,' replied Arni.

'Even when the land is hard as iron, everything is ice and snow and Skadi and her wolves roam the white frozen land?'

'Yes,' said Arni exasperatedly.

'Then tell me Arni, if everything freezes in winter including all inshore waters like this pond, how does the dragon appear?'

Arni looked at Odo.

'Because the pond we are looking for doesn't freeze in winter,' said Odo. 'If we can find that pond then there is a better than even chance we have located the pond the dragon lives in.'

'This pond does not freeze in winter,' said Nevena,

who had just returned from speaking with the old druid.

'I knew it,' said Odo clapping Arni on his shoulder.

'Does this mean that I don't have to dive down and search the pond's bed?' asked Siegfried who had been following the conversation.

'I don't think so Siegfried. Just put your hand in the water and tell me what you feel,' asked Odo.

Siegfried did as he was asked and was pleasantly surprised.

'The water feels warm and soft,' he said.

'It will,' said Odo.

'Why does the pond not freeze in winter?' asked Siegfried.

'From where I come from, in a place called Stave, we have waters that stay warm all year round even in the harshest of winters. Our wise men tell us it is because our god Surt, the destroyer, needs access to fire in his fight to cleanse the world with burning flame. These fires burn deep within the earth and keep water that bubbles out from underground springs warm where it forms into pools on the surface. I'm guessing this pond is just such a pool, warmed by Surt's fires. For a fire breathing monster such as a dragon this would be the perfect place to live.'

The lady Nevena looked at Odo with surprise and respect.

'I had no idea you were so well versed in the ways of the world,' said Nevena.

'I may look a brutish warrior but one of my uncles was a seer and taught me much,' said Odo smiling.

'So, what do we do now my lord?' asked Arni.

'Pray to Odin that I'm right and keep a watch.'

Chapter Fourteen

For two weeks the small Viking band kept a watch day and night on the pond without success. The druids were beginning to resent their presence and the men were getting bored and fed up with the inactivity. Ingvar in particular was railing against the lack of progress.

'Brother, I suggest we abandon this mission and seek riches and glory elsewhere. We are wasting our time here.'

'I have given my word to the high chief Cadeyrn and we shall see our mission through,' replied Odo.

'Is it for Cadeyrn or the lady Nevena that we remain?' asked Ingvar acidly.

'The lady Nevena has nothing to do with this quest other than as a well-informed member of Cadeyrn's council.'

'Humph,' said Ingvar unhappily.

Odo decided to rotate his men sending all but Siegfried back to Thorvald and Skidbladnir.

'Arni, keep a close eye on Ingvar and his followers. I can't afford to have him do something rash.'

‘You can depend on me,’ replied Arni.

Before the men departed Odo took his brother aside and told him that Arni was his chosen deputy and that he needed to take good heed of his leadership and command. This was somewhat superfluous as Arni was the most feared warrior among the forty strong band and was not a man to cross. Ingvar gave no indication either way of his feelings. He was just glad to be leaving the druid enclosure.

The following day Thorvald arrived with Hakon, Hastein, Bodvar, Erik, Haefnir and Leif.

The change in mood was instant as the new men were glad of the change from guarding their longship and were in upbeat mood at the chance of some activity.

With their arrival Odo decided that the time had come to take the initiative.

‘Siegfried, I need a volunteer and as our best diver and swimmer I’m looking at you. You don’t have to accept but we need to provoke this beast into action. Would you be willing to dive down into the pond and see if you can stir it into life?’

'Assuming, of course, it dwells within,' said Siegfried.

'I have no doubt of that,' said Odo. 'We will secure a rope to you so that should you get into difficulty we can pull you up fast. If you need to come up quickly tug the rope, sharply, twice.'

Siegfried had no choice but to agree. He didn't want to appear scared in front of these men nor be branded a coward.

Before Siegfried entered the water Odo set some of the men to clearing the deep surface layer of algae from the pond. A small round coracle, a Celtic vessel, was fetched from the coast by one of the men who had accompanied the lady Nevena. This enabled the Vikings to successfully rid the pond of all the algae, leaves and scum that had built up on its surface. The transformation was remarkable. The water shone and, while dark, was clear and the men could see a long way down.

The sight of this cheered Siegfried up. He hadn't been keen to enter the water when it was covered with thick green looking slime.

A long rope was attached around Siegfried's waist

and he slipped into the water.

'This makes a change to the other pond. It's so warm and pleasant,' said Siegfried.

'Good. Now let's be about our business,' said Odo.

With that Siegfried swam into the centre of the pond and duck dived down into the depths. His white body shone plainly through the water until it was but a small, indistinct white blob. A minute later there was no trace. Two more minutes went by and the men on the pond's bank became anxious.

'Shall we pull him up?' asked Hakon.

'No, leave him be. He can stay under for many minutes,' replied Odo.

Thorvald, who was holding the rope, suddenly lurched forward as he received two violent tugs.

'Pull him up Uncle, quickly now,' commanded Odo.

Thorvald hauled on the rope as rapidly as he could, assisted by Erik and Leif.

Siegfried's head broke the water and he swam swiftly to the side of the pond where he was helped out by Hakon and Hastein. He was trembling and not from the cold.

'I saw it Lord, red eyes glaring at me and a big gaping yellow mouth with vicious looking teeth. It was a frightening sight. His head appeared out of a hole in the side of the pond's wall.'

At that moment there was loud beating sound as a sinuous body broke the surface of the water and thrashed it into foam. Only the monster's body and tail appeared writhing around on the surface of the water. Several seconds later its head reared up and it fixed its beady red eyes on the men gathered around Siegfried on the bank before disappearing into the depths and the surface of the pond became calm again.

'So, we have our dragon,' said Odo satisfied. 'That was bravely done Siegfried. Take this. You have a true warrior's spirit and have earned it.'

Odo removed a ring of gold from one of his arms and presented it to Siegfried. This was a mark of huge respect among the Vikings. A man who wore a gold arm ring presented by his lord was a man to be reckoned with.

'You may be a Celt and you may be young but you have the makings of a true Viking warrior. I'm sure Odin will welcome you to Asgard when your time comes.'

'I hope that will be many years in the future young Siegfried,' smiled Thorvald clapping him on the shoulder.

Odo assembled his men around him.

'We have our dragon, we have his attention; all we need to do now is wait for him to come out of his lair and onto dry land.'

The men retired a small distance from the pond and watched and waited. There was no sign of the beast.

As the evening drew in the men lit a fire and sat down around it to consume a meal prepared by Bodvar.

'We've missed your cooking,' said Odo. 'I'm glad you accompanied Thorvald.'

As nightfall descended Odo set the watch, two men to be replaced regularly. It was during the third watch of the night when Haefnir shook Odo awake.

'The monster appeared my lord but only briefly. His head broke the surface of the pond but he just watched us for several seconds before disappearing.'

Odo roused the rest of the men but they spent a fruitless night hoping the dragon would reappear.

This routine continued for three more days and nights with the dragon only appearing on the third watch of each night. On the morning of the fourth day, after the beast first appeared, Odo decided that a new approach was needed. This time it did not involve Siegfried, for which he was grateful.

Odo approached the druid dwelling and asked to speak to the Lady Nevena, who had taken up residence in one of the druid guest huts.

'My lady, we have reached an impasse and need your help.'

'How can I, a mere woman, help seasoned warriors like you?' she asked, a smile wreathing her lips.

'We need a bait to lure the creature out of the pond and history tells us that this particular ogre likes to attack women.'

The smile disappeared from the lady Nevena's face. She was silent for some seconds.

'You want me to be that bait?'

‘I realise it’s a lot to ask, but yes I do.’

‘Assuming, for a moment, I agree to be the bait, how will the monster know I’m there?’

Odo described the behaviour of the dragon over the past three nights, how it appeared during the third watch and just gazed at the men ashore before disappearing into the depths of the pond.

‘I think if it sees a woman, particularly one as beautiful as you, it will be tempted to come ashore and investigate. You will be quite safe as I and the rest of the men will be close by.’

The compliment was not lost on the lady Nevena.

‘Hah! You think sweet words will get you what you want?’

‘Regardless of the monster and this escapade I think you are beautiful, from the first moment I saw you.

Nevena blushed but continued. ‘How close by will you be? If I am out in the open close to the water’s edge it will surely see big brutes like you if you are within a few feet of me.’

‘I have a plan for that. And the plan demands we have

our weapons with us. So, you must bring them with you from your dwelling.'

'I'm sure I can arrange that. What I cannot arrange is for your safety should anything happen to me. Both Cadeyrn and Badeyrn will demand justice with your lives.'

'Let me show you what I have in mind.'

Odo walked Neveva close to the pond's edge and described his strategy.

'I feel more confident now,' said Nevena. 'I'll agree to be your bait.'

Odo took Nevena's hands in both of his and squeezed them in gratitude.

'When do we undertake this venture?'

'Tonight,' replied Odo.

With that he turned away and issued a string of commands to his men who moved with alacrity.

'You think this will work Odo?' asked Thorvald quietly.

He was the only man who dared address Odo by his name as Odo was his nephew.

'It has to Uncle. I can't think of any other way. The

alternative is to sit here until it needs to leave its lair to seek more substantial forage than small fish, toads and weeds. But we could be here for a long time. The men will get restless and the hospitality of the Regni will be stretched.'

As night fell, Odo ordered Bodvar to prepare a hearty meal. A hog was roasted and the men were allowed a horn of mead. Once they had eaten and drunk their fill they settled down to rest. It promised to be a long and dangerous night.

At the beginning of the third watch the Viking band moved quietly to take up their positions. Instead of chain mail they all wore sturdy leather jerkins and leggings and had their faces darkened with mud. The fire had been stoked up and shone a warm, bright light across the glade. The only person not on the ground was Siegfried. He was perched up high in an oak tree overlooking the pond and it was his duty to signal the arrival of the monster in the middle of the killing ground that Odo had selected.

Across from the fire, some thirty feet from the pond's

edge, stood the lady Nevena in a pure white shift with her hair piled up high on her head. The glow of the blazing fire highlighted her form brightly.

Apart from Nevena the glade looked devoid of human life. She stood upright and still and began to sing an ancient Celtic ballad. She had a sweet, musical voice that carried clearly across the glade and beyond. As she sang she began to sway and move her arms. The effect on the watching Siegfried was mesmeric.

Nevena was half-way through her third song when Siegfried detected a ripple on the waters of the pond. A serpent like head with small ears rose several feet above the surface of the water. The dragon remained motionless with its red eyes focused on the swaying Nevena. The beast opened its mouth and a long forked tongue emerged flicking from side to side.

'Come on, come on,' muttered Siegfried to himself.

As if in response to his wish the creature began to swim towards the edge of the pond. It placed its front feet on the bank and pulled itself effortlessly ashore. It was big, some twenty feet of thick, coiled yellowish skin with four webbed feet and with small wings on its back. It began to move slowly towards Nevena who appeared not to have noticed its arrival. She continued to sway as she sang.

Nevena had seen the monster from the moment it had poked its head above the water but commendably she remained where she was, doing as she had been instructed. However, as the monster inched nearer towards her she was beginning to think Siegfried had fallen asleep. What was the boy doing and why wasn't he making the signal with his horn?

Siegfried with his overhead view could see exactly where the monster was and it needed to be a few feet further forward in the middle of the killing ground.

When Nevena was on the point of screaming the warning herself, Siegfried put the horn to his lips and gave a mighty blast. What followed next was complete mayhem.

The earth around the dragon erupted at four points as Hakon, Hastein, Erik and Haefnir miraculously appeared brandishing swords and yelling at the tops of their voices.

The dragon was taken completely by surprise. He looked left and then right before deciding it was time to secure his prey and drag it back down into his watery lair. But when he looked ahead, the lady in white had vanished to be replaced by a blonde giant in shimmering silver. Next to it stood a similar figure. The creature became angry, more so as Hakon had darted in and inflicted a deep gash on one of its legs. The other three men were attempting to do the same, slashing and stabbing their swords into the monster's flesh. The dragon reared up, looked to its right and spat a stream of purple venom straight at Erik who screamed and subsided to the ground. He began to swish his tail in a vicious side to side motion and one swipe caught Lief, who along with Bodvar, had broken out of the shrubbery on the other side of the pond and had come round to cut off its retreat. Lief dropped to the ground like a felled tree.

Siegfried, who was powerless to do anything, blew his horn as hard as he could to further confuse the monster.

Though he didn't know it, this was the dragon's undoing. On hearing the shrill horn above his head he looked up for its source, ready to spurt another jet of purple venom in that direction. This gave Odo the moment he was waiting for. He stepped forward, close to the dragon, and with one mighty swipe from his legendary sword, Dragon Slayer, lopped his head clean from his body. The dragon twitched and kept swishing his tail but as the men stood well back its motions gradually subsided until it fell to the earth unmoving.

'Well done all,' cried Odo, 'now, let's tend to Erik and Lief.'

Lief had suffered no more than severe bruising and a broken arm, but Erik was in a poor way. His leather clothing had prevented severe injury to his body and legs but his arms and head were suffering from third degree burns inflicted by the purple venom.

'My lady, where are you?' shouted Odo. 'We need your ministration and the healing skills of your druids.'

Nevena, who had rushed forward the moment the dragon had been slain, was standing right behind Odo.

‘I’m here my lord. I’ll see what can be done.’

Nevena organised for two of the druid brethren to take Erik into their enclosure.

‘He will be well cared for there,’ she said.

Odo, satisfied, called for Bodvar to place more wood on the fire and to break out more mead. The men had earned it and, god knows, he needed a drink. The dragon was bigger and more dangerous than he had anticipated and he hadn’t enjoyed placing the lady Nevena at risk.

The men relaxed and talked over the action.

‘That was a good ruse digging those pits opposite each of its feet and covering us with rush mats,’ said Hakon, ‘though I didn’t like being buried so close to it and not able to see what was happening.’

‘It was a good plan my lord,’ said Thorvald, ‘and thankfully it worked because of Siegfried in the tree. That was a master stroke, to keep blowing that horn. It provided the distraction we needed.’

Siegfried bowed his head.

‘I didn’t do much really.’

‘As for you my lady, that was bravely done,’ said

Thorvald, 'you have nerve I'll say that for you.'

'I was beginning to think Siegfried had fallen asleep and was about to scream, but the horn blast came in right on cue,' she said.

'Are you all right my lady, not too shaken?' enquired Odo.

'I feel better now I have some mead inside me,' she laughed, 'but it's not something I would like to be doing every day.'

As the fire subsided, the men settled down to sleep.

Nevena, instead of returning to her hut, insisted on sleeping next to Odo. She knew she would have a troubled sleep and wanted him close by.

Chapter Fifteen

'My lord, we have visitors,' said Bodvar standing over Odo who awoke instantly, 'the lord Cadeyrn and some of his hearth troop'.

Bodvar had been on the last watch of the night and as the sun had risen had started to prepare breakfast when he heard and saw their arrival.

'By Thor's teeth, their visit can't be acoincidence,' said Odo to Thorvald who, along with the rest of the men, had shaken off the cloaks they had been sleeping under and were getting fully dressed.

As Odo turned to seek out the lady Nevena he saw she had vanished from where she had been sleeping alongside him. That was a relief.

'So you have good news for me,' a voice boomed out. It was Cadeyrn who was striding towards them accompanied by two of his men.

'I have my lord. The dragon has been caught and slain. Your people need fear no longer.'

'That is well done. You must tell me how you accomplished the task.'

'Join us for breakfast and we'll tell you about the catching and the killing,' said Odo.

As Cadeyrn and the rest of men settled themselves on an assortment of wooden logs Odo recounted what had taken place. The Celts, like the Vikings, enjoyed a good story and Odo was adept at telling a good tale. Bodvar supplied hunks of bread with bacon and cups of watered mead which they consumed while they listened.

Odo gave a faithful account of what had taken place ensuring that each of his men were mentioned and praised. The only aspect he omitted was the part the lady Nevena had played in the capture.

'It was Siegfried's blowing of the horn high up in that oak tree that attracted the dragon and distracted him at a vital moment giving us the chance to deal it a killing blow.'

'I must see this creature,' said Cadeyrn getting to his feet.

The men had removed the body and head from the open ground into a pit they had dug deep in among the trees. Cadeyrn marvelled at its size though he pointed out they could grow to more than thirty feet in length. Odo was thankful he and his men had not had to deal with a fully mature dragon.

'Now, I must see my sister Nevena. Has she been helpful in this endeavour?'

'She has indeed my lord,' replied Odo.

As Cadeyrn turned to go, Odo asked him something that had been puzzling him.

'How did you know we had slain the beast, it was but hours ago and yet you knew?'

'The druids told me.'

'The druids?'

'With the aid of messenger birds, pigeons.' Cadeyrn went on to explain.

'This is new to me but powerful magic,' said Odo. 'You must show me.'

'Come with me now and I will,' he said, setting off for the druids' dwellings.

Cadeyrn strode into the druid enclosure and asked for the man who looked after the pigeons. He appeared, bowed, and was asked by his Lord to show them where the pigeons were kept. Odo noted a number of birds that seemed quite tame sitting within separate wooden cages. Cadeyrn showed Odo the little silver cylinders that housed the messages which were attached to a pigeon's leg.

'The idea is not new, and I believe originated in Arabia many centuries ago. Our holy men borrowed the idea and found that certain of our wild pigeons have a homing ability, meaning that they will generally return to their nest and mate.'

'How far will they travel?' asked Odo.

'Many hundreds of miles I believe,' said Cadeyrn. 'With these pigeons, and the druids who handle them, I can keep informed on what goes on across my lands.'

Odo was impressed.

'Come now,' said Cadeyrn, 'Your task here is finished and no doubt you would like to return to sea.'

'There is the small matter of payment,' said Odo.

Cadeyrn threw back his head and laughed. 'I am about to dispatch the lady Nevena to my dun to retrieve what is owed you. She and some of my men will bring it to where your boat is moored at the barrow by the ford. She should be back by tomorrow. Tonight, we will hold a feast in your honour and on the morrow we will bid you farewell.

**

Odo, and the men who had aided him in slaying the Regni dragon, were pleased to see Skidbladnir again. It was mid-day and the sun shone out of a cloudless sky. The high chief Cadeyrn and two of his men had gone hunting in a heavily wooded area nearby to furnish Odo and his crew with some fresh meat for their journey.

The Vikings were either tending to their gear or sitting in groups on the bank playing games and talking. They were relaxed, happy and looking forward to returning to sea. The lady Nevena was expected in the afternoon with their gold. The Vikings intended to spend one more night encamped on the shores of the river before leaving Regni territory.

As the afternoon wore on Odo became increasingly concerned. Call it a sixth sense but something didn't feel right. He shared his concerns with Arni and Thorvald.

'You fret too much man,' said Arni. 'She's capable, has the pick of Cadeyrn's men with her as escort and is in the middle of the Regni's kingdom. What could possibly go wrong?'

'Nevertheless, I trust Odo's instinct. It has saved our skin on many occasions,' said Thorvald.

'I'm wondering if your feelings for the good lady Nevena are not clouding your thinking,' said Arni with a mischievous smile on his face.

'I do care for her, that's true,' replied Odo seriously. 'But I have that prickle at the back of my neck which tells me something does not bode well.'

'It's early yet and the Lord Cadyern doesn't seem concerned,' said Arni.

Cadeyrn who had just returned with a deer slung over one of his horses seemed in a relaxed mood and had set his men to skinning and preparing the beast for cooking and salting as a way of supplying preserved meat for the Vikings for their journey.

By early evening, though, he began to share Odo's concern.

He summoned one of the two men who had accompanied him on the hunt, Seisal the scout.

'Seisal, I want you to ride back to my dun and find what is keeping the lady Nevena and get back here as soon as you can.'

'Yes, my lord.'

It was mid-summer and not dark till late into the evening. Seisal had more than enough time in which to complete his ride on a fresh, quick horse.

Some time later the sound of a horse being ridden fast towards the Viking camp on the bank of the river brought the men to their feet. It was Seisal. He looked grim and the horse was lathered with sweat and foam. Seisal brought his mount to a shuddering halt and leapt from his saddle. He went straight up to Cadeyrn and knelt before him.

'Bad news my lord, the lady Nevena's convoy was attacked, most of the men killed and of the lady Nevena and the gold there is no sign. It happened but a short distance from here.'

Before he could continue Cadyern interrupted him.

'You said most of the men were killed. Was anyone left alive?'

Two men my lord, one is unconscious, and only the gods will decide whether he lives. The other, Aedan, was left for dead but had regained his senses when I arrived. Though bleeding heavily, I believe he will live.'

'Who would dare to attack my men on my land?' thundered Cadeyrn. 'They were good men, strong warriors. How did this happen?'

'Dumnonii warriors my lord, at least twenty, too many for the six hearth men with the lady Nevena. They were taken completely by surprise. It looked a well planned ambush. Our men acquitted themselves well, killing twelve of the Dumnonii. But the odds and the surprise were too great.'

'Dumnonii! What are they doing here so far east and how would they know about the convoy?'

'That I do not know my lord.'

'You have done well Sesial. Get yourself a drink and some food. I need to think.'

Listening to the exchange was Catha, one of

Cadeyrn's captains of horse. He ventured an opinion.

'We should go after them immediately my lord. The longer we leave it the greater their chances of escape.'

'They timed it well Catha. It will be dark soon and we cannot track them in the dark, whereas they can push on. They are already well ahead on the trail.'

'We could at least try my lord.'

'That we can Catha. Take all the available men here and set off after them. Leave Seisal and Guern. I will need them. I will send word to our cousins the Atrebates. You should have no problem tracking across their lands. The Durotriges will be a different matter, but leave that to me.'

'I'm on my way my lord.'

Odo, who had remained silent up to this point, spoke calmly to Cadeyrn, even though his senses were reeling. The lady Nevena was in the hands of bandits, the gold he and his men had put their lives on the line for was gone and he felt helpless.

'If there is anything we can do to help my Lord, you have but to ask.'

'There may be Odo, but something is not right about this. How would the Dumnonii know about the convoy? They must have been informed but by whom? This is a puzzle that needs thinking through.'

'Who are the Dumnonii my lord?'

'Cave dwellers and pygmies from the south western most reaches of our isle. They consider themselves above their fellow Celts because of the tin they mine and its distribution which they control. As you know, tin is an extremely valuable commodity used in making weaponry, tools, jewellery and fine utensils for both practical and decorative use. It is said that, as a result, they are the wealthiest of our tribes, apart from maybe the Ordovices who mine the red welsh gold.'

'If they are so wealthy, why would they come this far to raid for gold?'

'A good question, but you should know that there are many factions among the Dumnonii and some of the princes are not so wealthy. They may own land but their land does not contain the valuable tin mines and their king rules ruthlessly. He has many sons and he fears that they may rise up and usurp his throne. So he keeps them shackled, as best he can, and controls carefully who manages the mining and distribution of his tin.'

Odo was not minded to hear about Dumnonii politics. He was more concerned with the welfare of the lady Nevena and the gold that the Vikings had worked hard to obtain.

Cadeyrn interrupted his thoughts. 'I will think on this over night and tomorrow we will decide how best to use your offer of help. Right now I need to smooth the way for Catha and his men across the territory of the Durotriges and consult with the druids.'

Odo watched Cadeyrn walk away shouting for Guern to attend him.

Siegfried and the Vikings - 'The Dragon and the Witch'

Chapter Sixteen

Siegfried awoke early and decided to explore the woods nearby. Though he didn't like to admit it to himself, he was feeling a little homesick and being among the trees reminded him of home. He liked being with the Vikings and still trained every day with sword, shield and spear, and practiced his Norse with Karl, but the relative inactivity and the chores that went with being the youngest member of the band were beginning to bore him.

He collected one of the bows the Vikings possessed and set off to see if he could, at least, bring back a rabbit, or two, for Bodvar to cook. There was no doubt that Bodvar's cooking was better than his mother's.

He set off quickly and soon reached the tree line. Not far in among the trees he came across a warren on the edge of a clearing and hunkered down to wait for a rabbit to appear. Some minutes later a large rabbit emerged from one of the burrows and sniffed the air carefully, eyes darting from side to side. Siegfried took up the tension of the bow string, sighted along the arrow shaft and was about to release the goose feathered shaft when a movement across the other side of the clearing sent the rabbit scuttling back into its burrow. Siegfried cursed silently and sank down onto his stomach, well hidden in the tall grass.

Five men appeared and squatted down in a circle. One of them pulled out a large roll of bread which he tore up and distributed among his comrades. Siegfried recognised Ingvar and Rolf but couldn't see the others easily without giving his position away. He could clearly hear what they said though.

'You all know the situation we are in. Our gold has gone, Leif and Erik have been injured and my brother fawns upon the Celtic chieftain because of his lust for the lady Nevena. We are sitting around on our backsides waiting for him to make a decision. I say it's time we took action,' said Ingvar.

'I don't like it anymore than you my lord, but what is to be done?' replied Rolf.

'Action Rolf, that's what I demand. I believe we

should seek our gold here then leave these shores.'

'How shall we do that my lord?' asked one of the other men.

'Did you not see the gold in Morcant's hall? The vessels the food was served in, no doubt for Badeyrn and the lady Nevena's benefit, were of solid gold and are worth a tidy sum on their own and no doubt there is more gold in his coffers.'

'But your brother would never agree to such an action,' said another.

'I wasn't thinking of asking for his permission dolt,' replied Ingvar. 'He would never agree. But if we could secure the gold and bring it back to Odo, I feel sure he would be pleased and then we can leave. I also asked Aun for a prophecy and it was favourable.'

'You told Aun of your plans?' said Rolf.

'Not exactly, I gave him enough of the gist of what I intended.'

'But there are not enough of us to go up against Morcant's men,' said Rolf.

'That's true my friend, so it's Loki like cunning we will

have to employ and I have been thinking of a plan that could work.'

Ingvar relapsed into silence chewing on a mouthful of bread.

'Well, are you going to share your plan with us?' asked Rolf.

'One of us will approach Morcant just before dusk and give him a message from Cadeyrn. The message is that he and his men must leave immediately for the dun of the Atrebates king to meet Catha to aid him in his quest to retrieve the lady Nevena and Cadeyrn's gold. They have tracked down the Dumnonii bandits but there are too many of them for Catha and his few men to fight. He needs Morcant's support.'

'Why wouldn't Catha enlist the support of the Atrebates king and his warriors?' asked Rolf.

'Politics and, fortunately, Morcant is an impetuous man not imbued with high intelligence. If the lord Cadeyrn has commanded him to ride, he will.'

'Surely, Morcant would expect this message to be delivered by one of Cadeyrn's men and not one of us?'

said one of the other men.

'He would but we will explain that Cadeyrn's men have set off after the Dumnonii and that Cadeyrn himself is busy negotiating with the Durotriges, in case the bandits escape Catha. The only alternative was to send one of us.'

'It might work, but I'm not so sure' said Rolf reluctantly.

'Are you challenging me Rolf? For, if you are, we will settle the matter here and now,' said Ingvar getting to his feet and drawing his sword. 'I can't abide disloyalty, and that goes for the rest of you.'

Rolf and the others remained where they were, keeping their eyes focused on the ground. Ingvar glared at his men before sheathing his sword and squatting back down. They were used to Ingvar's outbursts and how to deal with them.

'When do we put this plan into effect my lord?' asked Rolf.

'Tonight,' said Ingvar. 'Right, let's go. We have to determine our tactics and we need an excuse to leave the camp during the afternoon. The five of us should be more than enough to make our scheme work. I will deliver the message to Morcant. He is more likely to believe me as Odo's brother.'

After the men had departed the clearing Siegfried waited for a long time before getting to his feet and silently and swiftly heading back to the encampment; all thoughts of hunting rabbits forgotten.

**

As Siegfried entered the outskirts of the camp he saw that Cadeyrn and two of his men were riding toward the Viking encampment. Siegfried watched as Cadeyrn dismounted and immediately sought out Odo.

'I know where the Dumnonii scum are taking the lady Nevena, your gold, and who put them up to this and I know how you and your men can help me, if you are so minded.'

'You have been busy my lord. How do you know this?'

'One of the Dumnonii was still alive when we got to him and told us what we needed to know. It took some persuasion but I have men who are skilled in extracting information. He was a cousin to the prince who led the raid and sang his heart out before he departed this world.'

Odo grimaced but was keen to know what Cadeyrn had found out.

'In Dumnonia there is a sacred place known as Tormohun. It contains a series of ancient caves that go back to before time began where a sorceress, Gwrtheyrna by name, dwells. She is said to be old as time herself. She practices the dark arts and is protected by two demons that are terrifying to behold. She holds great power over the Dumnonii and it is said while she lives the prince, who is her protector, will prosper. She demands only two things, gold and beautiful young women, the more high born, the better, who she offers up as sacrifice to her gods.'

Alarm raced across Odo's face.

'You asked if you could help, my lord Odo. So, you can. Kill this woman and her demons, return the lady Nevena safe and sound and not only will you have my gratitude and that of the Regni people, you will have more gold than you safely carry aboard your longship. Tormohun is on the south coast of Dumnonia and the caves close by the sea. In a fast ship like Skidbladnir you should reach it before the Dumnonii war party. From what I have seen, this is a venture you and your men are uniquely gifted to undertake.'

'You make it sound easy my lord. What do we know of the Dumnonii strength in the area of the caves?' Odo asked.

'The renegade prince has his dun about two miles from the caves on the south west shore of a small peninsular. The caves are to the north east. They are situated in the cliffs above the sea.'

'Can an approach be made from that side?'

'That I do no not know and will be something you need to find out. Seisal tells me that there is a small cove at the foot of these cliffs but his memory is hazy.'

'How would Seisal know this?'

'He knows the ways of the Dumnonii. His grandmother was from their people. I will ask him to accompany you.'

'How many fighting men does this prince of the Dumnonii command?'

'Fifty at least, but he can call on others that owe allegiance to his brothers.'

'Before I agree to this mission I must put it to my men,' said Odo.

'The Viking way, eh?' said Cadeyrn.

'Indeed my lord.'

'I will await your decision then, but let us hope it is the right one,' said Cadeyrn grimly.

Siegfried saw his chance and ran up to Odo.

'My lord, I have something important to tell you.'

'Not now Siegfried,' said Odo brushing him aside as he called out for his men to gather on the shore beside Skidbladnir.

Siegfried was about to call out after Odo, who was walking towards the longship, but noticed that Ingvar and Rolf were close by. His news would have to wait.

Odo addressed the assembled Vikings and told them what had passed between him and the lord Cadeyrn.

Several of the men asked questions. The discussion

went on for some time. Ingvar had said nothing up until this point, but he now spoke.

'Brother, we have survived a great storm, we have slain an evil beast, two of our band have been injured and we have nothing to show for our efforts. I say it is time to end this quest and not go on a wild goose chase where we might lose more men and still come away empty handed.'

Rolf and a couple of others nodded.

'I say we demand payment from the lord Cadeyrn for the slaying of the dragon and then be on our way.'

Several others, mostly men who were sworn to Ingvar, grunted their agreement. Prominent among them was Aun, whose view carried a deal of weight.

'You forget that the Dumnonii now have the gold we were promised,' said Arni.

'Aye, that's true,' replied Ingvar, 'but the Regni have much gold. We were promised payment and payment we should have. The lost gold is the lord Cadeyrn's problem, not ours.'

'What of the lady Nevena?' asked Arni.

'We have fulfilled our side of the bargain and the Celts should honour theirs. The lady Nevena was not part of the bargain and she is not our concern.'

'But without her help we could not have accomplished the slaying of the dragon,' pointed out Arni.

'So you say, but our allegiance is not to her, it is to ourselves and the task we undertook.'

The argument went back and forth for some while with other men venturing their opinions. Odo took no part in these discussions, neither did Thorvald.

Finally Odo spoke. 'I have heard enough. Unless anyone has anything else to add I suggest it's time we decide.' Odo looked enquiringly around the assembled men but the Vikings fell silent.

'Uncle, please distribute the bones.'

Thorvald reached into a bag he was carrying and handed each man two slim bones. They resembled small sticks with one being shorter than the other. Each man knew what to do. This was an ancient tradition used to determine the path the Viking band would follow. The long bone represented agreement to the course of action proposed by their leader; the short one disagreement. A bag of blue material was placed on up-ended bole of wood. Each man had to place one of the two bones they held in the blue bag. The remaining bone was to be placed in a mustard coloured bag on an adjacent piece of wood. Whatever the outcome, no-one would know who had voted for, or against, the proposed course of action. The bones in the blue bag would be counted with the greater number of longer, or shorter, bones determining the decision which was binding on all present. If anyone disagreed, or felt uncomfortable with the outcome, they could leave. This rarely happened.

The bags were laid out at a short distance and each man walked up to them and placed his bone of choice in the blue bag with the other going into the mustard coloured one.

Cadyern watched the proceedings with interest and scepticism. This type of leadership was alien to him and would not be the way he would lead. Democracy was not something the Celts practiced.

The bags were brought to Thorvald and Ingvar who moved away from the men. Thorvald undertook the first count, Ingvar the second.

'Are we in agreement Ingvar?' asked Thorvald.

'We are,' said Ingvar.

Thorvald announced the results.

'We sail for Dumnonia.' This was greeted by a cheer from the bulk of the Viking band.

Odo smiled at Cadeyrn and went across to speak to him.

Siegfried, who had been patiently waiting for his chance, saw Odo deep in conversation and, after the last rebuff, wasn't sure he could interrupt. Thorvald, however, was standing on his own having just issued instructions to a number of the men. Siegfried saw his opportunity.

'Uncle, I have something important to report to you and the lord Odo.'

Thorvald turned his gaze upon Siegfried and smiled.

'What is it young man?'

'Treachery uncle, Ingvar and his men plan to rob the

lord Morcant of his gold and they intend to do it this evening.'

'How do you know this Siegfried?'

Siegfried related all that had taken place in the woodland beyond the Viking encampment. Thorvald listened carefully, asking a couple of questions.

'You have done well Siegfried. We now need to inform our lord. Come with me,' whereupon he turned around and walked purposefully towards Odo.

Odo was not happy at being interrupted in his conversation with Cadeyrn but as it was Thorvald he knew it had to be important.

'I need to speak with you my lord, alone' said Thorvald.

'As we are united in a common mission, and I trust the lord Cadeyrn, I'm sure you can speak in front of him,' replied Odo.

'Not on this occasion my lord.'

Cadeyrn, who sensed the gravity of Thorvald's message, excused himself.

'Well Uncle, what is it?' asked Odo, more than a little

irritated.

'It concerns Ingvar my lord.'

Thorvald went on to repeat what Siegfried had told him and asked Siegfried to retell his story. Odo listened intently before speaking to Thorvald.

'Uncle, I apologise for my rudeness, the forthcoming trip is taxing my powers of patience and thought. Ingvar, always the impatient one; he has been sent to test me, a test I may fail one day, but not today. I had intended that we sail on the high tide this afternoon but we must delay our departure till tomorrow. Inform the men and ask Bodvar to cook a good meal tonight with plenty of mead. I'm sure the lord Cadeyrn will oblige with the food and drink. This is what we must do about Ingvar,' said Odo.

Thorvald listened intently and nodded.

Chapter Seventeen

Following the vote, Ingvar approached Thorvald who had just finished outlining Odo's plans for departure to the men.

'Uncle, we will need many supplies for the forthcoming trip. I thought Rolf, I and a couple of my men would spend the afternoon hunting. More fresh meat cannot hurt.'

'A good idea Ingvar, may Ullr, our god of hunting, guide your hand.'

Ingvar turned away and gathered Rolf and the others around him. They collected two bows and their spears and headed off into the trees. Once in the tree line, Ingvar motioned them to stop and outlined, again, what he intended.

Rolf spoke. 'But, my lord, the men have voted, and we sail for Dumnonia, the gold and the lady Nevena. Surely, we do not need to put ourselves at risk with this venture.'

'Listen, if we can bring enough gold to satisfy the men and my brother, we will have no need to embark on such a foolhardy enterprise. The men will see this, and we can put the decision to another vote which I'm sure will be in favour of us not heading off to Dumnonia on a fool's errand. My stock with the rest of the men will rise and then we'll see who comes to lead this band; any further questions?'

Rolf, while not certain this was a good idea, had sworn allegiance to Ingvar, as had the other men present, so relapsed into acquiescent silence.

'Very well, let's go.'

They pushed deep into the woods until they came across a well worn track that they knew would take them to Morcant's dun. When they came within sight of the settlement they halted and watched. All appeared quiet.

'Rolf you remain here. Any sign of trouble and you and the other two come swiftly. Sagtha, you're with me.'

Sagtha was a big surly man, of limited thought. But he was immensely strong, good with sword and spear and the ideal man to guard one's back.

He was loyal to Ingvar and did as he was told.

Ingvar left the trees and walked confidently towards the gated entrance to Morcant's dun.

There were two men on the gate who stepped out in front of Ingvar and asked him his business.

'I'm here to see the lord Morcant, on the high lord Cadeyrn's orders,' he said.

'And who may you be?' asked the older of the two men.

'I am Ingvar, brother to Odo, the dragon slayer, and I am here with his blessing as well as the lord Cadeyrn's.

The men parted and the older one asked him to follow. He set off towards Morcant's hall. If Ingvar thought this was going too smoothly, he didn't show any sign of it.

At the hall the older man bade him enter and said he would return to his duties on the gate. The settlement seemed quiet with few folk abroad. A couple of children played in the dirt outside a dwelling and several dogs were scratching themselves in the dust.

Ingvar pushed at the heavy door and, followed by Sagtha, entered the dimly lit hall that smelt strongly of a pleasant smelling smoke. His eyes took a while to adjust to the subdued, hazy light. The hall appeared empty though he couldn't fail to notice that the long trestle table contained several eating and serving vessels of gold that appeared to be laid out for a feast. He touched Sagtha on the arm and nodded at them.

At the far end of the hall he could make out a large, grand and carved chair, Morcant's chair, with its back to the door and he could vaguely make out a figure sitting on it. Standing by the chair facing him was a Regni warrior. Ingvar called out.

'My lord Morcant, I am Ingvar, the brother of Odo, the dragon slayer, and I come with greetings from your lord Cadyern. The lord Cadeyrn wishes me to convey a message to you.'

The Regni warrior spoke. 'Greetings lord Ingvar and what would the message be?'

'Your high lord Cadeyrn wishes your lord Morcant and his men to leave immediately to assist in apprehending the Dumnonii bandits who absconded with his gold and the good lady Nevena.'

'Indeed,' said the warrior. 'And how would you like to respond my lord Morcant?' he said, turning to the person in the chair who began to rise and turn to face Ingvar.

Ingvar's face registered shock as he took in who was standing before him.

'Greetings brother,' said Odo.

Ingvar was speechless but while his mind was dulled his right arm moved swiftly, drawing his sword which he pointed at Odo. Sagtha followed likewise, neither of them knowing exactly what they would do now their swords were drawn. The Regni warrior had disappeared behind a curtained screen in the corner leaving them alone.

'What trickery is this brother?' said Ingvar. 'Is it really you standing before me, or have the druids cast a spell on me? It's so dark and smoky in here I can barely see or think.'

'It surely is me Ingvar.'

'God's blood, I hate this damp, misty isle with its demons, witches and sorcerers. But sorcery aside, I think

I have you at a disadvantage brother. I don't know what you are doing here, or where Morcant and his men are, but it seems to me that now is a good time for a reckoning.'

'Exactly what did you have in mind?' enquired Odo.

'Ceding leadership of Skidbladnir and our band of men to me would be a start. Secondly, you can help me gather up all the gold that is on display here plus whatever else we can find in Morcant's coffers once he and his men have left to follow Cadeyrn's orders, which will be so much better coming from you. We can then leave this isle without going to its farthest reaches in search of this witch and her demons.'

'And what if I should not agree with your plans?'

'I may be no match for you in one-to-one combat, but between myself and Sagtha, the strong, I fancy you have no chance. You will do as I say, or suffer the consequences.'

'Sagtha is indeed strong, but not as strong as me,' spoke another voice as the flat side of a large war axe whistled through the air striking Sagtha on the back of his head, whereupon he slumped unconscious to the ground.

Ingvar turned to find Arni gazing at him malevolently. Odo smiled and spoke.

'You were saying brother? I suggest you put your sword aside and come and sit down here with me to discuss this matter further.'

Ingvar knew when he was beaten and reluctantly dropped his sword to the ground which Arni collected. When both men were seated, Odo continued.

'I knew you would be trouble when I agreed to take you on this odyssey, but our dear mother insisted. If not for her I would happily feed you to Ran and her daughters. I promised to take care of you, her favourite, but brother you push my patience. I want it understood that you will give me no more trouble and that you will acknowledge my leadership and follow my lead.'

Ingvar said nothing.

Arni tapped him on the shoulder with his huge war axe. 'Speak Ingvar. While our lord Odo made his promise to your mother I am under no such obligation,' he said menacingly.

'All right, all right,' said Ingvar. 'It shall be as you say.'

'On your knees Ingvar and swear allegiance to me in Odin's name,' said Odo.

Ingvar did as he was commanded.

'Good, now we shall say no more of this and what has passed here will remain between the three of us. Arni, fetch some water to wake up Sagtha and then let us get out of here back to Skidbladnir. Ingvar, you will speak with Rolf and the others and I expect to see you back at the ship before us. Do I make myself clear?'

'Yes brother.'

'Yes, my lord!'

'Yes, my lord.'

'Good, now be on your way. We'll bring Sagtha with us.'

Ingvar departed, wondering how Odo had come to know of his plans and arrive at Morcant's settlement before him. He could barely breathe from the smoke and was certain an evil spirit had thwarted him.

Once Ingvar had departed, the curtain parted and

Cadeyrn entered the hall with the Regni warrior that had stood beside Odo earlier.

'That was well done. Though, if he'd been my brother, I would have punished him more severely.'

'I made a promise to our mother, one that I will keep. I am sworn to look after him and protect him,' said Odo.

'A burden indeed,' said Cadeyrn.

'Now perhaps we can get on with our voyage, but first we have an evening meal to attend to with my men, so let's be on our way,' said Odo.

Chapter Eighteen

'Look lively there,' shouted Arni at a Viking who was clumsily attempting to push the prow of Skidbladnir away from the bank.

'Raise the sail and may Njord favour us with his breath, otherwise it will be a long row to the sea boys,' Arni commanded.

As if on cue a breeze sprang up and filled the cream coloured sail. The Viking band was in high spirits, pleased to be going back to sea and not having to pull on their oars.

The journey down river was uneventful and soon the longship was in open water and riding the waves southwards with the men pulling powerfully at the oars.

Agnar, the steersman, had the tiller and was intent on taking their craft due south for some distance before turning onto a westerly heading.

The journey westwards was uneventful. The wind blew steadily from the south easing their passage as the big, single sail captured the available breeze and powered them along. Agnar remained on the tiller and kept the south coast of Britain just in view on the horizon.

Siegfried spent much of his time high up the mast keeping a watch on the surrounding sea for any signs of other craft. Apart from a broad beamed ketch, likely a merchant's vessel, pitching eastwards through the sea close to land, he did not see another ship.

As night drew in, they headed inshore looking for a suitable point to land and make camp for the night. Seisal proved his worth with his knowledge of the coastline and the local country; for though they were in the country of their allies the Atrebates, it paid to be careful, quiet and watchful.

That first night passed uneventfully. The following night would see them beaching in the territory of the Durotriges, potentially a different proposition altogether if they were observed coming towards the coast. For this reason Odo had the men lower the sail some way out at sea and insisted on them taking up their oars to pull them ashore. Without the huge billowing cream sail with its red dragon markings showing up against the blue of the sea and sky, Odo was trying to present as inconspicuous a profile as possible to any likely watchers on the land facing them.

Fortune appeared to favour them as they ran their longship up onto the shingle without any welcoming committee. However, to be certain, Odo, as always, had a party of men leap overboard as soon as the ship was close to the beach to set up a protective screen on the shore in case of any trouble. Once the ship was grounded Odo had three pairs of men set off east, north and west to scout out the lie of the land.

Their arrival appeared to have gone unnoticed.

Soon Bodvar had a fire going and a stew of game and vegetables bubbling over the flames. Siegfried, who had been practicing his Norse with Karl, appreciated the smell and his stomach was rumbling in anticipation.

'Siegfried, over here,' commanded Odo.

Siegfried walked across to where Odo was standing by the prow of Skidbladnir with Thorvald, Arni and Sesial.

'I need you and Sesial to keep the first watch tonight

in case we attract any visitors. Your Celtic is local and far better than any of ours and it may be sufficient to deter any would be inquisitors. If challenged, you say we are on a mission from the King of the Regni on its way to Dumnonia. No need to go into any lengthy explanation. If pressed, say you know no more than that. You will operate separately at either end of the beach we are on, up there in the bluffs above. I will have two of my men with each of you; one to help you in case of trouble, the other to return here to warn the rest of us. Am I clear?'

Siegfried and Seisal both nodded.

The first watch passed peacefully enough, as did the other watches and at dawn the Vikings were on their way out to sea.

However, the clear weather, which had blessed them so far, had vanished. The sky had a leaden look with the sun trying to shine through a haze of yellow grey cloud.

'This does not bode well my lord. Like as not a sea mist will descend very soon,' said Agnar to Odo.

'We'll have to take our chances Agnar, for time is against us. We must press on.'

It was Karl at the top of the mast who noticed the sails first.

'Two ships to our starboard stern my lord,' he cried to Odo, who looked up at him.

Odo gazed back at the shore and could see two squat looking vessels, each carrying two sails, heading towards them but still some distance away.

'By the lord Odin, they are making good speed through the water. Agnar, what do you make of them?' said Odo.

'Celtic vessels made of oak with two leather sails each and in a wind they will out sail us my lord,' he replied.

'Durotriges, I'll be bound. Arni, get the men to their oars,' commanded Odo.

Even with oar assisted power the Viking longship with its single sail could not outhaul the two Celtic ships, which closed the gap remorselessly. Arni had set a hard pace for the oarsmen and they were beginning to flag. They couldn't keep this up for much longer.

The two approaching ships were now almost within arrow distance and it soon became clear that that their intentions were not friendly. A volley of arrows was launched at the Viking vessel. All fell short into the sea but it was a gesture of what they intended.

Odo called out to Arni. 'Arni, we are outnumbered two to one in terms of warriors and they will be upon us soon. Unless the gods intervene on our behalf this is my plan,' he said.

Siegfried, who was facing the oncoming ships, began to get alarmed and called out to Karl who sat at the bank of oars across from him.

'Karl, they are out pacing us and will soon be upon us.'

'Fear not Siegfried, our lord Odo will know what to do and Aun will be working his sorcery.'

'Aun,' spat Siegfried. 'I wouldn't place hopes of our survival on that weasel!'

Aun was, at that moment, working himself up into a terrible frenzy at the rear of the longship. Shouting incantations to the heavens and curses at the oncoming ships he held a large animal's thigh bone in his right hand which he banged hard on a brass vessel every few seconds. Spittle was flying from his mouth as he kept up his tirade that carried clearly across the water to the oncoming craft despite the wind and sound of the sea.

Whether it was Aun's invocations, Agnar's reading of the weather or the gods taking pity on the Viking ship, the wind started to drop and a mist began to form over the sea.

The advantage now moved to the Viking ship as their oar power began to tell. The Celtic vessels began to fall behind and, as the mist thickened, they vanished completely. The sea became as calm as a mill pond and the main sail hung limply.

'Arni, have the men stop rowing,' commanded Odo. 'We need complete silence.'

In the thick mist every sound was amplified and the Celts could be heard cursing not far away.

'We should row while we have the advantage,' whispered Agnar.

'No, the sound will give our position away,' replied Odo. 'We'll drift awhile. This mist looks set to stay.'

'I can't argue with that,' said Agnar. 'It will be with us

for some time and will delay our arrival in Dumnonia.'

'Better that, than dead at the hands of these Durotriges cut throats.'

Odo also knew that his men badly needed a rest from what had been a back breaking period of rowing. Many of them had bleeding hands and several were feeling dizzy and light headed.

Enjoying the respite the Viking crew sat still with their arms resting on their oars listening out for any sound from the Celtic vessels.

The Celtic shouts had died away but still Odo insisted on complete silence. Just as he began to relax, a huge shape loomed out of the mist on their starboard quarter as one of the Celtic vessels sliced across their prow without seeing them. The men tensed and more than one reached for their long swords and began to withdraw them from their scabbards.

'Quiet,' hissed Arni. 'Do you want to wish these heathen upon us?'

The men concerned froze where they were and quietly as possible slid their weapons back into their sheaths.

The cat and mouse game went on for some time before Odo deemed it safe. The fog continued to hang over them, hiding their position from the Celtic vessels, and Odo asked Arni to have the men begin rowing.

Siegfried was puzzled and leant across to Karl.

'We can row, but we could be rowing around in circles. How do we know what direction to travel in?' he asked.

'Agnar has the answer; it's powerful magic,' replied Karl.

As if on cue, Agnar retrieved a small wooden box from under the rear awning of the longship. He opened the lid and withdrew a fist sized chunk of yellowy orange stone. Its four sides tapered to a rough point which Angar clasped in his hand.

Despite the mist the stone shimmered as it caught the available light. Agnar held the stone above his head and peered at it intently. There were many layers of light but one was stronger in colour than the others and appeared as beam passing from one side of the stone to the other. From the way the beam lay, Agnar could work out the position of the invisible sun and, hence, determine the direction they needed to be rowing in. He handed the crystal to Odo who would hold it aloft while the mist remained so that Agnar could ensure he steered the longship in the right direction.

'We need to go about my lord,' said Agnar.

'Arni, you heard him. Get the men to put their backs into it,' said Odo. We need to put some distance between us and the Durotriges scum and make up for lost time.'

As the men began to pull at their oars with renewed vigour, Agnar adjusted the tiller in line with direction the crystal showed him.

They rowed blind for some time before the fog began to lift and much to Siegfried's amazement the southern shore of Britain was just visible on their starboard side. And best of all there was no sign of the two Celtic ships.

'I told you it was powerful magic,' said Karl.

'I believe you. But what is it and how does it work?'

'That lump of rock is known as a crystal moonstone

and came into Agnar's possession from Arabia. That's all I know. You'll have to ask Agnar or Odo how the magic works,' replied Karl.

'I know the gods are all powerful,' said Siegfried to Karl, 'but this is some wizardry. Agnar has managed to keep us on course and evade the Durotriges.'

'I'm sure the gods have something to do with it,' replied Karl, 'but Agnar knows what he is doing and he is the best sailor there is. There is magic in that stone which, he alone, can determine.'

As the fog lifted, the wind increased, the sail billowed and Arni commanded the men to ship their oars. Skidbladnir slipped easily though the waters headed west to its destination.

Chapter Nineteen

It was late afternoon as a light wind propelled the longship through a deep blue sea that sparkled in the sunlight. Odo had gathered Thorvald, Arni and Seisal around him at the stern of the vessel close to where Agnar held the steering oar.

'Seisal, by our estimation we will be upon the coast of Dumnonia by early evening. Your lord mentioned you know of small cove close to the caves where the sorceress and her demons reside. Is it suitable for us to beach and lie up over night?' asked Odo.

'My memory is hazy lord, but I believe the cove contains a sandy beach and is of a size for us to land securely.'

'What makes you say securely?'

'The cove cannot be reached from the land. It dwells at the bottom of tall cliffs.'

'That should suit our purpose well.'

'Is that wise Odo, given we need to find a way up to the caves? Would it not make more sense to find a beach where we can more easily strike inland? It would also cut our movement down should we need to take to sea and reconnoitre for another landing point' said Thorvald.

'That makes sense Uncle, but this cove lies almost directly under the witch's cave and I'm hoping we may yet find a path. Seisal is not so clear in his recollection.'

'It's a risk.'

'Aye it's a risk Uncle, but given what we have just come through, the omens feel good and I believe Odin favours our venture.'

'So be it,' replied Thorvald.

'Seisal, how many fighting ships can the Prince of Tormohun muster, where are they based and how long before they could get to us in the event of discovery?'

'If you mean ships like those of the Durotriges, the Dumnonii do not possess such craft.'

'Then how do they organise and protect their trade in tin?'

'They rely on merchants from Gaul and the other Celtic tribes to come and purchase their tin and take it away in their vessels. The tin is of such value they see no need to invest in building ships of their own to trade the tin away from Dumnonia. These same merchants also bring goods in exchange that the Dumnonii need.'

'What about their fishermen?'

'Aye, the Dumnonii are a tribe of fisherman, but they operate small sailing boats to catch fish in local waters. The fish is in such abundance around the cliffs and promontories they have no need for larger sea going vessels.'

'That reduces one area of threat,' said a satisfied Odo turning to Arni.

'Not if some local fisherman decides to set his nets in the waters of the cove we are heading for,' he replied.

'You better pray to Odin that he doesn't Arni. Now let's reef the sail to half its size. I want to delay our arrival until just before sunset. Once the cliff tops are in sight, we row in. And relieve four men from the rowing, the ones with the sharpest eye sight to survey the cliffs. I want to know if our arrival is spotted.'

It was evening and the sun had dipped behind the towering cliffs as Skidbaldnir slid quietly onto the sandy shore which faced east. Men flooded ashore to secure the beach and haul the front quarter of the longship up onto the sand. Their arrival had appeared to have gone unnoticed.

‘Seigfried, Karl, come,’ called out Odo. The two boys gathered round him.

‘Unless the rabbits around here are the size of goats, I believe goats have visited this beach,’ said Odo, holding out his left hand which contained many tight round black balls of manure.

‘Where there are goats, there will be a path. I want you two to see if you can find it before night fall. Apart from your knives don’t take any weapons. You will need to be nimble. If you encounter anyone, hide if possible, and then get back here as fast as you can. Understood?’

The two boys nodded and set off to explore the perimeter of the cove. The left side of the shore, where they had beached Skidbladnir, was overshadowed by a massive, limestone cliff. A path up that side did not look likely. Towards the right the cliffs were not so sheer and were lower in height.

'Let's try our luck over there,' said Karl.

At first glance it did not appear that there would be a path, especially as a number of huge limestone boulders were gathered above the beach around the base of the cliff on that side. Siegfried and Karl, however, persevered in their search and found a way through. Once at the base of the cliff they spotted a narrow path that was clearly used by goats. It cut its way diagonally upwards across the face of the limestone cliff towards the east which, as they climbed, became shallower in slope. Within a short space of time they were on the top of the cliff overlooking the beach. The longship and the Viking crew appeared in miniature below, though they were heavily over-shadowed by the towering cliffs on the other side of the cove.

'Look at the view eastwards over the sea; it's breathtaking,' said Siegfried.

'Never mind the view. We need to ensure there are no Dumnonii hereabouts,' replied Karl.

Both boys looked around and found a well-worn path that circled the cove before striking off westwards.

There was no sign of any human presence, no dwellings, no old fires and no goats.

'The area appears completely deserted,' said Siegfried.

'Aye, it does,' replied Karl.

No sooner had they spoken than the sound of a tinkling bell reached their ears.

'Quick, over here behind these thorn bushes,' hissed Karl.

Both boys dropped to their stomachs. They watched as an elderly goatherd, a wizened looking man, appeared with a number of goats clustered around him. The biggest goat had a piece of leather tied around his neck which held a small brass bell. The boys watched as the man and his goats disappeared along the path towards the west.

'That was a close call,' said Siegfried.

'It was,' replied Karl. 'Now let's report back to our lord.'

'You've done well,' said Odo, 'but we must keep an eye open for the goatherd. He could sabotage our expedition. Now get something to eat. Siegfried, after you have eaten come and join me under the cliffs over there.'

Whilst Siegfried and Karl had been scouting the path some of the men had made a grim discovery in the corner of the cove under the towering cliffs on that side, human bones. Some were relatively recent, and all looked as if they had been gnawed at by wild animals. There was no obvious reason for them being there until one of the men down by the water's edge gazed upwards and spotted a sizeable opening in the cliff face half way up from the beach.

'Perhaps this is something to do with the sorceress, Gwrtheyrna,' remarked Thorvald, upon being told of the bones and inspecting the spot for himself along with Odo.

'Whether it is, or it isn't, Uncle, it's too high for us to explore and the cliff face is too sheer to climb,' said Odo.

All of the men around him muttered and reached for their amulets and good luck charms. There was evil in the air. They all moved well away from the spot as dusk fell.

The evening was balmy helped by the sun warmed limestone that towered over them as Siegfried joined Odo, his closest companions, his brother and Seisal by a large boulder that had once been part of the cliffs overhead.

'Despite our brush with the Durotriges and losing time due to the sea mist, by Odin's good grace we will have out-run the Dumnonii prince and his men. Tomorrow, I want you, Seisal and Siegfried, to visit the prince's dun. Seisal, you speak the local dialect and need to invent a suitable story for visiting this part of Dumnonia with Siegfried. I want to know the strength of the warriors there, whether they patrol this headland, the mood of the people and, if the prince has out-ridden us and returned, where he might be keeping the lady Nevena. God forbid she hasn't already been handed over to the witch in the caves above. The rest of us will find the main entrance to the caves and check the lie of the land. Once we have a clearer picture, we can determine what must be done. Are we all clear?'

The men around Odo nodded.

'And, Seisal, acquire two large fishing nets the kind the Dumnonii trawl for fish with in the sea.'

'Yes, my lord,' replied Seisal.

Night fell as the men settled down to sleep. A pair of men set off up the path, guided by Karl, to take the first watch. The night passed uneventfully until dawn when a squawking human voice in an unfamiliar tongue reached the ears of the men on the beach who were at their breakfast.

It was the scrawny goatherd who Siegfried and Karl had seen earlier. Seisal translated for Odo's benefit.

'He asks Cocidius to piss on you.'

'I take it Cocidius is one of their gods?' asked Odo.

'A Celtic god of war my lord,' said Seisal.

'Well he has pluck. Now tell him we mean him no harm, that he will be our guest a while, and find out from him where the main entrance to the sorceress's cave is. And once you have accomplished that I need you and Siegfried away as quickly as possible to the Prince's dun.'

'Yes, my lord.'

It was mid-morning before Seisal and Siegfried set off for the settlement of Tormohun. Siegfried was dressed in rough peasant's clothing with just a knife strapped around his waist. Seisal wore a leather jerkin and carried his sword but no shield or spear. Both carried leather satchels that contained water, food and some coinage. To the casual eye it would appear that they had travelled from afar and arrived at the village on foot.

Following the path west they eventually came across the outskirts of the Prince's dun, a collection of round thatched huts situated on a westerly facing slope that ran down to the sea. A stout wooden palisade surrounded the village and there appeared to be only one gate in from the landward side. Two of the Prince's household warriors stood either side of the gate looking bored while two others briefly examined those entering. There was a queue waiting to enter the settlement.

Seisal greeted the older of the two men in the local dialect and after a fleeting look he waved them both through the gate.

In the middle of the village was an imposing hall made of large lengths of oak with a thatched roof. It was an impressive building and fit for a king never mind a prince of the Dumnonii.

It was market day, which explained the queue outside, and meant that the settlement was thronged with many visitors from the surrounding countryside as well as the locals. The market occupied the square in front of the hall and just behind the stalls was a tavern dispensing mead and what passed for the local ale.

'That's where we will find out what we need to know,' said Seisal pointing, 'as well as getting some much needed refreshment.'

Seisal and Siegfried managed to secure a perch on one of the wooden benches outside the tavern and asked a skinny serving girl for two beakers of ale.

Seisal was soon in conversation with a burly man who sat next to them. He was a carter who transported goods. As a result, he knew most of the merchants in Tormohun and, as luck would have it, enjoyed exchanging gossip. Seisal soon learnt that the Prince was away with most of his men on some business and that no-one knew when he would be back. This was welcome news.

Seisal also learnt that the Prince was not much liked by his people and had recently increased local taxes on all those who lived and worked within his domain.

Having bought the carter his next drink Seisal turned the conversation to the sorceress, Gwrtheyrna. The carter's face took on a grim look.

'You sound like a local man, but I take it you are not from these parts?' queried the carter.

'My mother married a man of the Regni and I have been away a long time but I vowed to return to see my grandmother, who is still alive, to bring her news of my mother and to look over a small property that will be bequeathed to me,' replied Seisal.

'You would do well to settle your business and be gone,' said the carter, who then lowered his voice. 'The Prince is in thrall to that witch who demands ever more gold and sacrifices. The gods be praised that I do not have a young, winsome daughter. At least one young woman every two months is dragged forcibly from her family's hearth by the Prince's men and given to that harridan to feed to her monsters. Any resistance is met with instant death.'

'The people here look cheerful enough,' said Seisal, waving his hand at the crowds.

'Aye, on the surface, for folk have to live and enjoy life as best they can. But underneath, this is a cursed place and many would leave if they could. And don't be abroad at night. The witch's demons roam the land and devour anyone they come across.'

Siegfried, who had been listening, had begun to lose interest in the discussion. His attention was taken with a juggler who had set up his stall in an open part of the square and was juggling several multi-coloured balls in front of him, behind him and through his legs. This was far more interesting. He got up and left Seisal to his inquisition. Seisal, absorbed in his conversation, did not notice his departure. As Siegfried left to watch the magician there was a clamour at the gates.

The prince of Tormohun had returned.

Chapter Twenty

Siegfried was in the middle of the square when he heard the sound of heavy horses. He looked up and saw a band of men headed by a young, grand looking man with a red cape, riding their horses directly towards him.

Along with other villagers, Siegfried moved to escape their path. As he moved aside, he looked up and saw the lady Nevena on a white mare. Before he could think, he called out.

'My lady!'

Unfortunately for Siegfried, the Prince heard his cry and immediately reined his horse in. He looked down at Siegfried and spoke to a burly man mounted on a horse next to him.

'Seize that boy and bring him with us!'

The big man leant over and plucked Siegfried off the ground as if he was a feather and slung him on his stomach across the front of his horse. Before Siegfried could say anything, the party moved swiftly towards the prince's hall where they dismounted.

Siegfried was taken into the hall and placed in a small

room at the back where one of the prince's men was left to guard him. Siegfried cursed his stupidity.

After what seemed a long time the door was opened and the prince entered the small room.

'So, what have we here?' asked the prince.

Siegfried looked up sullenly and kept quiet.

'If you wish the lady Nevena to remain unharmed you'd better speak up boy. Now, where are you from, how do you know the lady in question and what are you doing here?'

Siegfried had been thinking of his cover story from the moment he had been incarcerated.

'I'm of the Regni, my lord, and the lady Nevena is sister to our king. My uncle is of your people and had to pay a visit to his grandmother and asked if I would accompany him. This I did and we arrived here this morning. I wasn't expecting to see the lady Nevena here in Tormohun.'

'This is an unlikely tale. How would a peasant boy like you know the lady in question or what she looked like?' the prince demanded.

'Only last month our king Cadeyrn and his sister came to our village. I was chosen to serve food and drink to our guests in our lord's hall. The lady Nevena spoke to me and I would recognise her anywhere,' replied Siegfried.

That information fitted with what the prince knew of their movements before he had captured the lady.

'Your uncle, what is his name and where was he when you last saw him?'

Siegfried saw no harm in providing this information as he knew Seisal would be long gone.

'Seisal, my lord, and I last saw him drinking ale in the tavern on the square.'

The prince turned to the man who had grabbed Siegfried and ordered him to go and find him. As the big man left, the prince turned to another of his companions.

'Keep the boy here and don't let anyone speak to him.' With that command he stalked off.

Sometime later Siegfried heard footsteps and the door opened. It was the prince and the big man.

'It seems your uncle has vanished into thin air boy. What kind of uncle is he not to make enquiries about your whereabouts?'

Siegfried kept quiet.

'Tell me your story again?'

Siegfried repeated what he had already said and told the prince about his village.

'Enough boy, I don't want chapter and verse on life in your miserable settlement.'

Siegfried lapsed into silence.

The prince turned to the big man. 'Take this boy to Aud the slaver. There's an auction in two days' time. He should fetch a good price and remind him that I'm still waiting for my commission from the last auction. Tell him to remove the boy's tongue. I want nothing said about what has taken place here, nor of the lady Nevena.'

The big man nodded.

**

Seisal, who had witnessed the taking of Siegfried, had left the tavern immediately and headed away from the main gate towards the sea. As he had hoped there were no guards on the gate that led onto the shore. He headed for the beach where several fishing boats were drawn up and quickly found what he was looking for. Several nets had been left out to dry. He grabbed two and bundled them up tying them tightly with leather thongs. There was no-one about as the fishermen were all at the market selling their catches. So far, the gods were looking down favourably upon him.

He headed rapidly along the shore as far as he could go and then ascended upwards into the tree line. Following the headland round he was soon above the cove where the Viking ship was beached.

Shortly after that he was relaying what he had seen to Odo, Thorvald and Arni. He began with Siegfried's capture and then went on to describe the general mood among the people, their view of the prince and the increases in taxation. Odo returned to the prince's arrival.

'You're sure it was the lady Nevena?' asked Odo.

'It was my lord.'

'By Thor's hammer we have to rescue the boy,' said Arni.

'We will Arni, I just need some time to think how,' said Odo.

Thorvald spoke up.

'We need information Odo. We need to find out exactly where Siegfried is being kept and also the lady Nevena.'

'That should be easy uncle. I warrant they are being held in the prince's hall. But, as you say, it would behove us to be sure.'

Odo turned away and asked the nearest Viking to fetch Osric, the Gaulish trader.

'Osric, I need you to become the trader and merchant you are in the Dumnonii settlement on the other side of this headland. Your task is to find out where Siegfried and the lady Nevena are being held and, if possible, what the prince's plans are for both. We know the lady Nevena is to be given to the sorceress, Gwrtheyrna, and by Odin I hope that hasn't happened yet. Seisal tells me that it's a three day market so the prince's dun should be heaving with people and gossip. Take Arni with you. With his red hair and a change of clothes he could pass for a Gaul. He can play the part of your body guard.'

Arni was delighted to be going, a welcome change to their current inactivity.

Osric and Arni set off not long after. It was late afternoon and, though the market would be drawing to a close, the traders and villagers would be embarking on a night of feasting and drinking. Osric and Arni wanted to be part of that, for drink made for loose tongues.

They approached the same gate that Seisal and Siegfried had gone through earlier in the day.

As before, two of the Prince's household warriors stood either side of the gate. This time there was no queue waiting to enter the settlement.

'A little late for the market?' questioned one of the men.

'Ay,' replied Osric, 'our horse went lame and we had to leave it and the cart with my other man at the next settlement up the coast. We have come ahead to ensure that all the best goods are not all sold by the close of the market.'

'So, you have nothing to sell?'

'We do, Frankish blades, Greek earthenware and Roman wine. My man should be here by mid-day tomorrow. This is a three day market?' enquired Osric.

'It is, so Gauls are you?' asked the guard spitting onto the ground.

'We are from Samarobriva,' replied Osric.

The guards looked at Osric and then Arni, who impressed them by his height, bulk and red hair twisted into a solid plait down his back, and let them both pass into the settlement.

'So far so good,' said Osric, 'let's find a tavern where we can spend the night and then we can see what there is to be gleaned from the good people of Tormohun.' Arni nodded his agreement.

All the taverns were full but at one rather seedy looking place off the main square there was room in the hay loft above the stables. Osric agreed terms with the landlord and handed him two heavy looking silver coins of Frankish origin. The landlord immediately became friendlier.

'If there is anything I can do, lord, to help your stay here you have only but to ask,' the greasy looking man said.

'You can start by telling me about the market, the most common things bought and sold and the level of commission levied on the merchants by your lord?'

The landlord told Osric what he knew and was dismissed. He and Arni then left the tavern in search of more information, drink and food.

**

Siegfried sat upright as he saw the door open to the room where he was being held. Two men came in with leather thongs in their hands. They twisted Siegfried's arms behind his back and attempted to tie the thongs around his wrists. Siegfried reacted violently. He kicked one man hard on his shin and head butted the other. Both men had under-estimated Siegfried's strength. Though still a boy, the daily practice with weapons under the Vikings' tutelage had built up his power, speed and agility. He was slippery as an eel and twisted out of the men's grasp. He ran for the door and would have been through it and away if he had not run straight into the big man who had first captured him. The big man held him easily.

'So, the boy tries to escape does he? You idiots, can't two of you handle a mere boy and truss him up securely?'

'He's stronger and faster than he looks,' one replied.

'No excuses. Tie his wrists and hobble his ankles. Our lord will skin us alive if we let him escape.'

Siegfried was subdued and, with a rope securing his ankles together, shuffled along between the men.

He was taken out of a back door to the hall which was close to a network of alleys that ran between thatched round houses. He quickly became disoriented. Within a short space of time he was pushed through the low entrance of a rectangular building which was unusual amongst the round houses common to the settlement. Facing him was a thin man with a scarred face.

'Here he is Aud. My master wishes you to sell him,' said the big man.

‘A fine looking specimen, and of a good age’ said Aud, ‘I imagine we will fetch a top price for him.’

‘There is a condition,’ said the big man, ‘his tongue must be removed; otherwise there is no sale.’

Aud, the slaver trader, protested vehemently declaring the boy would be worth a lot less without his tongue.

‘If you value your life and wish to continue to live and trade profitably here then you would be wise to heed the wishes of our master,’ said the big man.

Aud, realising this was no idle threat acquiesced. The three men delivered Siegfried into Aud’s care. Behind Aud stood two of his minders who looked like the thugs they were.

‘What’s your name boy and where are you from?’

‘Siegfried and I am of the Regnii,’ Siegfried said proudly.

‘Such a lovely voice too,’ said Aud, ‘a pity we will have to remove your tongue and an even greater pity as it will seriously reduce your value.’

He turned to his men and ordered them to place

Siegfried within one of the holding pens at the back of the big building, where he appeared to be on his own. That had also been a stipulation of the prince. He did not want Siegfried speaking with anyone, not even another slave, and the sooner his tongue was removed the better.

It was late when Aud returned alone to the slave pen.

'I don't know what you have done to incur the wrath of our lord, the prince, for you seem a well-made and intelligent youth, for a Regnii.'

Siegfried just gazed back at Aud.

'And, if you wish to use your intelligence I would strike a deal with you, if you are interested?' said Aud.

'Go on,' replied Siegfried.

'You will fetch a handsome price at auction, but without your tongue you will be worth much less. Ahead of the auction, which takes place in the market square, I conduct a private viewing for certain clients. If I let you keep your tongue you must keep your mouth shut, curb your temper and go nice and quietly when you are sold. I have a particular client in mind from the Ordovices. He will treat you well and is far enough away from here for our lord prince not to discover that I have disobeyed him. Do we have a deal?'

Siegfried, who wanted to keep his tongue, agreed. He had been praying hard that Seisal would have got word back to Odo and that he and his men would be searching high and low for him, though how they would find him here he did not know. But he had to keep his spirits up.

**

By good fortune, Osric and Arni were drinking with some of the prince's household warriors who were taking bets on the outcome of an arm wrestling match between Arni and one of their number, an ugly brute of a man called Osferth. While not as big as Arni, he had an impressive set of biceps and was the undisputed arm wrestling champion of the Dumnonii.

Bets were placed and Arni and Osferth sat down on benches, facing each other across a table, and shaped up to the challenge ahead. They clasped hands and waited for a slim man with a big nose, who was the referee, to start the contest; a match that would be the best of three.

'Go!' shouted the slim man.

Both men took up the strain and began to heave away. For many moments neither right arm wavered. Then with a sudden shout Osferth punched his hand and arm to his left and began to over-power Arni. He began to exert his considerable strength and pushed Arni's arm over until it hovered just above the table. However, Arni held him there. Several seconds went by as Osferth strained away until sweat began to bead his forehead. Even for a man of his power he could not keep up the pressure and had to relax his grip. As soon as he did, Arni counter-attacked and brought his arm to the vertical, where he held the grip of Osferth. A cat and mouse game ensued where neither side gained a particular advantage.

Men began to shout and cheer, with the majority supporting Osferth. As the shouting reached a particular crescendo, Arni gave an almighty bellow, which would have frightened the gods out of their beds, and slammed Osferth's arm and hand to the table; round one to Arni.

Both men took a break and sipped ale while speaking with their comrades, in Arni's case Osric.

'Take it easy Arni, we don't want to upset these turds,' said Osric quietly.

'Don't worry, I have everything under control,' replied Arni.

Following the outcome of round one, the odds on Osferth shortened and all new bets were placed on Arni, apart from one which was placed on Osferth by a greasy looking man.

And so round two began. Things proceeded much as before with neither man gaining a particular advantage. After a couple of minutes Osferth appeared to relax and let Arni move his arm to his right. Osferth then relaxed his arm completely which took Arni by surprise and as he hesitated Osferth smoothly exerted all the power he had and slammed Arni's arm over onto the table; round two to Osferth. His supporters went wild with excitement.

'That's better,' said Osric, 'now don't let your ego get in the way in the final round.'

Arni just grunted.

After another drink, round three commenced. The third round followed the pattern of the previous two with first one man gaining the advantage and then the other. As the round continued, Arni appeared to be breathing hard and blowing through his mouth.

'Too much for you Gaulish?' called out Osferth, 'you seem to be tiring.'

Arni ignored the jibe and concentrated on keeping his hand and arm firmly clamped around Osferth's. However, his arm began to tremble with the exertion and Osferth sensing his chance put everything he had into one swift and powerful move and slammed Arni's arm onto the table.

The room went wild and Osferth's supporters slapped him on the back and offered to buy him a drink.

Arni turned away and looked at Osric.

'Well done,' said Osric, 'you had me worried there.'

'I hate losing,' growled Arni.

'It's all in a good cause,' replied Osric, 'and you know you can beat him. So, relax and let's get chummy with these bastards.'

Osferth was feeling magnanimous. 'You were a tough opponent Arni, the best I have encountered in recent months. Let me buy you and your comrade a drink and come and join us.' This was exactly what Osric and Arni wanted.

As the night wore on they were drinking, laughing and joking easily with the Dumnonii warriors. As they drank they learnt more about the prince, about his recent captive the lady Nevena, what would happen to her and about the boy who had been seized. The man who told Arni and Osric about Siegfried's immediate future was one of the two men sent to bind him and take him to Aud the slaver.

'Slippery bugger he was,' the man said, 'but we got him to the slaver and on the prince's orders his tongue will be removed so he can't tell no-one about the lady Nevena and her fate. By this time tomorrow he'll have been sold off to some wealthy household at the slave auction, never to be heard of again.'

Osric and Arni kept their composure and enquired about the slave auction and where they might find Aud.

Osric said he would be interested in purchasing slaves to sell on in Gaul.

When they felt they had gleaned as much information from the men as possible, they bade their farewells and staggered off into the night.

On arriving at the tavern where they were staying, Osric shouted for their landlord who eventually appeared and handed over a bag of coin.

'What's that?' asked Arni.

'Our winnings from tonight,' replied Osric, slipping two coins to the greasy looking man.

'Winnings?'

'Yes, I asked the landlord to place some money on Osferth after the first round.'

'By Loki, that's cunning of you,' said Arni.

'I try and profit where I can,' said Osric, 'now, we have a busy day ahead of us tomorrow so let's get some sleep.'

Chapter Twenty One

The following morning Osric, with Arni behind him, was knocking at a small door set into the gate of a large rectangular building. A flap at eye level was opened inwards and a pair of eyes looked him up and down followed by a voice asking what he wanted.

'My respects to your master but I would meet with him,' stated Osric.

'Your name?' asked the person behind the eyes.

'Osric.'

'My master is not expecting you,' said the man.

'He is not,' replied Osric, 'but I would like to discuss a possible purchase of slaves with him.'

'The public auction is in the market place at the middle of the day,' said the voice and the flap closed.

Arni stepped forward and banged his mighty fist on the door several times shaking it severely.

The flap was opened again and the same eyes looked out. They widened when they took in the size and bulk of Arni.

'My master won't ask again,' said Arni fiercely, 'if you

don't open this door, I'll break it open.'

'It's all right Arni, I'm sure that won't be necessary,' said Osric, in a placating tone. 'I have personal business with your master. Please fetch him.'

The eyes weighed up both men. 'Wait here, I'll see if he can be disturbed,' said the voice as the flap was closed again.

Eventually, the small door was opened and both men were invited to step inside. Aud was facing them with two burly looking minders just behind him hefting ugly looking wooden cudgels.

'How can I be of assistance?' asked Aud.

'I understand that you conduct some personal sales ahead of the main auction,' stated Osric, 'and I would be keen to buy the best you have before the auction commences later today.'

'You are mis-informed,' replied Aud, 'now, if you'll excuse me, I have a busy morning in front of me.' He turned away as the two minders stepped forward hefting their clubs.

'Wait!' said Osric opening a purse that jingled with

coin that was attached to his belt.

He extracted a gold coin which he proffered to Aud. The merchant's eyes narrowed as he took the coin and examined it.

'There is plenty more of that should we be permitted to conduct a trade,' said Osric.

'I don't know you and you are very foolish to come here without an introduction,' said Aud, eying Osric's leather purse hungrily. The two minders moved closer.

Osric held out another coin to Aud. 'Keep the two coins as my introduction,' said Osric.

As Aud took the second coin, Arni moved swiftly towards one of the two minders. He disarmed him, broke his arm and knocked him to the ground unconscious.

'And that is my introduction,' said Arni, 'in case you get any ideas about relieving my master of his gold.'

Aud was shaken by how quickly Arni had taken care of one of his two body guards, men who were powerful and proven thugs.

'Arni, that's enough. Now, my lord, shall we conduct

some business, business that will be profitable to us both?' said Osric smoothly, seemingly unperturbed at what had just happened.

Aud, realising these were dangerous men, saw sense not to mention the chance to make a profitable sale. He smiled weakly and invited the two men into the main hall. He ordered the other minder to take care of his comrade.

'What exactly are you looking for?' asked Aud.

'I have a client in Gaul who is looking for a well-made boy and he is prepared to pay well for the right specimen.'

'I may have a couple that would suit your client,' replied Aud, who ushered Osric and Arni towards a number of cages lining the far wall of the hall. He showed Osric the two youths he had in mind. Osric did not appear impressed by either.

'I have an older boy over here,' said Aud motioning Osric towards another pen.

'I'm afraid he is too old for my client,' said Osric.

Arni nudged Osric, pointing towards a cage that was

at the far end of the hall where a dimly lit figure could be seen squatting on the floor.

'What do you have over there?' asked Osric.

'He is not for sale,' said Aud, 'he is promised to another of my clients who will arrive shortly.'

'Nevertheless, I would like to take a look,' said Osric walking purposefully towards the cage before Aud could stop him.

Osric arrived at the cage and peered inside.

'Stand up boy, so that I can get a good look at you,' commanded Osric. The boy did as he was told.

'Turn around. Now show me your teeth.' The boy did as he was told.

Osric addressed Aud. 'A healthy looking youth, riddled with lice but he will clean up. He will be ideal, how much?'

'He is not for sale,' said Aud again.

'Everything has its price and I'm willing to pay well for the right goods,' said Osric, waving his bag of coin under Aud's nose.

'I take it you are not from these parts?' asked Aud.

‘I am from Samarobriva and my client is in Gaul,’ said Osric.

Aud thought quickly. These barbarians were clearly from overseas and the boy would be gone with them. That would be an even better outcome than having him taken to the tribal lands of the Ordovices. He made up his mind and opened the negotiation with an eye watering price. Osric did not blink and countered with a much lower offer. The haggling went on for some time before they agreed an amount.

‘There is one further condition of sale,’ said Aud.

‘What is that?’ asked Osric.

‘That you leave the settlement within the hour. My client will be very upset when he discovers that I have sold this boy to you and I want to keep any possible repercussions to the minimum.’

‘I do have further business in the village but if you agree a discount of ten percent I can arrange to be gone from here within the hour.’

‘Very well, we have a deal,’ said Aud.

The cage was unlocked and the boy withdrawn. He

said nothing and looked sullen. Aud suggested a hood was placed over his head to hide his identity. Osric accepted the hood from Aud, placed it over the boy's head and retied his purse, now much reduced in weight, to his belt. He gestured for Arni to pick the boy up. Arni, without effort, picked him up and slung him over his shoulder. With relief, Aud showed both men out of another door that led out onto a maze of stinking alleys. He was glad to be rid of all three. Osric and Arni were just as keen to be gone.

They stepped out outside and swiftly disappeared into the depths of the village. With the knowledge gained from Seisal's earlier exit from the village, they set off for the gate that opened onto the shore. There were no guards on the gate and within seconds they were striding along the sand towards the wooded headland. Once they were well in among the trees they halted and Arni set the boy down. He disappeared back down towards the shore to check they had not been followed. Osric pulled the hood off the boy and cut the leather thongs that were binding his wrists.

'Let me take a good look at what I have purchased,' said Osric smiling.

Siegfried had tears in his eyes and was shaking.

'Thank you Osric. I knew you wouldn't abandon me,' said Siegfried, 'but I don't mind telling you I was frightened, particularly as they intended to cut out my tongue.'

Osric gave Siegfried a hug. 'That's all right lad. We always look after our own and, besides, Odo would have to answer to Arni if we deserted you. And, as powerful as Odo is, I wouldn't give much for his chances if he had to face an angry Arni. Now, we had better be going as we have the lady Nevena to rescue and a witch to slay not to mention her monsters.'

Arni reappeared at that moment. 'It's good to see you lad,' said Arni, clapping Siegfried on the shoulder, 'but we have trouble; four men heading this way. Aud's doing, I'd wager.'

'The man's a fool,' said Osric.

'We can't afford to let them get near the cove,' said Arni, 'which means we must take them here. This is what we will do.'

The four men entered the trees but had to come in pairs as the track narrowed. One of them called out, pointing at the ground on which glittered several gold and silver coins spread across a range of six feet. All four knelt down scrabbling to pick up the treasure. That was their undoing. Osric and Siegfried, each holding a sizeable chunk of rock, stepped out from the bushes either side of the path and brought them down on the heads of two men at the front. Arni stepped out from behind a large tree and grabbed the two rearmost men by their necks, picking them up as if they weighed nothing and cracked their heads together. All four men collapsed to the ground groaning. Before they could recover Arni expertly broke their necks. Siegfried looked shocked.

'We can't leave them alive lad. The cove is too close. Hopefully master Aud will count his blessings and now leave well alone. Help me drag them off the path towards the edge of the bluff through here.'

The bodies of the four men were pushed into dense

undergrowth overhanging the sea below. It would take a thorough search to find them. The coins were picked up and Arni used a fallen sprig of pine to sweep the path clean of their tracks.

'Time we got back to the cove. Let's go,' said Arni.

**

The Viking band was delighted to see the successful return of Siegfried. He had become a talisman for the crew and, like all Norsemen, they appreciated the story he told them.

As the men dispersed, Odo asked Seisal, Osric, Arni and Thorvald to remain behind. The subject under discussion was the lady Nevena.

'From what you have told me, the lady Nevena is to be sacrificed at the beginning of the festival of Lughnasa,' said Odo.

'That's right my lord,' replied Seisal, 'it's the festival that marks the beginning of the harvest in honour of the God Lugh. The Dumnonii believe that sacrifices need to be made to ensure continued fertility for their womenfolk as well as their crops. Their sorceress,

Gwrtheyrna, demands only the most beautiful and, ideally, high born are sacrificed. The lady Nevena is the perfect subject for their ritual.'

'When does the festival commence?' asked Odo.

'It varies year to year but from what I learned in the village, and Osric agrees, tonight will be the start of this year's festivities. For us Celts day begins at night. The moon is revered more than the sun, sacrifices are made at night and tonight the moon is full.'

'Tonight it is then,' said Odo, 'the longer we remain here, the greater the chances are we will be discovered. Once we have secured the lady and slain the witch's monsters we will be gone from here, and I mean tonight. Uncle, I want you to ready Skidbladnir. The sea is calm and we should have light enough for rowing. We will leave for the witch's lair at dusk. The goatherd says he can lead us to a secondary entrance to the caves; this should give us some small advantage.'

The men spent the afternoon sharpening their swords and axes. As dusk approached Odo asked Aun to cast his rune sticks, speak to the spirits and ask for their blessing on the undertaking.

Aun lit a fire, slit the belly of one of the goatherd's goats and studied the entrails. He worked himself up into a frenzy, shouting incomprehensible sentences, and behaved as if the very spirits were speaking through him. Perhaps they were. Most of the men stayed well away from him and touched their amulets and lucky charms. Finally, he cast the rune sticks and studied them for a long time. He then arose from his squatting position and approached Odo.

'The spirits have spoken lord, and they tell of darkness, fire, serpents and death.'

'Whose death?'

'The portents are not clear lord. They are clouded in mist. If I could perform the ritual with a human sacrifice they would become clearer. The Celtic boy among us causes trouble. I have no doubt the gods would look favourably on our mission and reveal the outcome if we could make that sacrifice, the ultimate offering. The mists would clear and the omens would be less obscure.'

'Out of the question Aun; touch him and I will

sacrifice you to Odin personally. Now leave me.'

Aun scuttled off muttering under his breath.

'I'm not sure it's wise to upset our rune master Odo?' said Thorvald mildly.

'I fear the gods as much as the next man, uncle, and I know if I touched one of their holy men I would be bound for Helheim not Valhalla but it's time Aun realised Siegfried is now one of us. He has earned the right.'

'I agree,' said Thorvald, 'come, it's time you entered the caves.'

As the light began to go, Odo led ten men, including Arni and Siegfried, up the path away from the beach. The goatherd was with them. Three of the men carried the nets Seisal had obtained and two coils of rope. One man carried a big bundle of dry driftwood. Dressed only in leather armour, chain mail being deemed too cumbersome, the men carried their favoured weapon. They were not anticipating running into any of the prince's household troops. For most of the men their chosen weapons were sword and dagger. Arni carried his big war axe and four of the men carried a number of spears in addition to their swords. One man carried a bow. Though archery was not a weapon common to the Vikings, Odo had long realized the value of having men in his crew who could shoot arrows into foes who threatened them on sea and land. Bows were also superior to spears when it came to hunting game for food.

Once on the clifftop the goatherd directed them along a path that led north east, away from the prince's dun. He brought them to the brink of a large cleft in the ground that was heavily wooded along its sides but held a clearing in the middle. The men all crouched down and Odo and Arni crawled to the edge and looked over. Looking west they could see a procession of men and women winding its way towards the clearing.

A group of men in white gowns, many with beards, led the procession chanting. These were their druids. Following them were men and women wearing garlands of berries and fruits. They swayed in time to the chanting of the druids and music that came from several pipes played by minstrels.

In the middle of the group was a tall, well-muscled man wearing a helmet of stag horns. Behind came three women in white shifts with their hands bound with leather thongs. One of these women was the lady Nevena.

Arni felt Odo bridle beside him and laid a restraining hand on his arm.

'Now is not the time, lord, to rescue the lady,' he said.

'I wish we could just go down there, take her and be gone from this land,' replied Odo.

'Look,' said Arni.

Behind the procession came a score of the prince's household warriors, all heavily armed. The last to enter the circle of men and women who had now gathered in the clearing below was the prince. He too, was wearing a simple white gown.

'It's time we entered the caves lord. Let's find this witch, kill her and her monsters and then we can rescue the lady,' said Arni.

Odo and Arni retreated from the edge and Odo commanded the goatherd to lead them to the secondary entrance to the cave complex.

To the ordinary eye it would be hard to find. The entrance was a narrow fissure that was concealed behind a screen of silver birch and scrub oak. The men pushed their way through the trees and vegetation and entered the caves.

Every other man carried a sheaf of tightly bound straw with its end dipped in oil which they set alight. The flickering flames cast a ghostly light on the limestone walls of the passage they entered.

The men followed the passage until it ended in a huge cavern. The men felt small in its vastness. Huge stalactites hung down dripping moisture onto the floor. Where the drips fell stalagmites had formed. The air smelt of damp decay but also of something else, an animal smell. Apart from the corridor they had come down three other passageways were evident leading into the cavern.

Odo's companions were hardened warriors but they felt fear. This was a place of hell and not a good place to die. Odo broke the silence by issuing instructions to the two men carrying the ropes. They were to explore the first passageway to their immediate right. With one torch between them the men departed.

'And mark your direction with cuts in the limestone,' commanded Odo.

The remaining men, with Odo leading, set out to cross the cavern. They were half way across when they detected a movement at the other side accompanied by a loud rasp. The men stopped and looked. Emerging out of one of the passageways was a dreadful looking creature. Standing on two legs was a leathery looking beast with a snake-like head and neck. Its head carried two fearsome looking horns and its legs were eagle-like, with huge curved-talons. Each rasp was accompanied by a gout of flame. In size the creature was not much taller than Odo.

'By Thor's blood, what is that,' cried one of the Vikings.

Spread out,' cried Odo, 'Erik, Ivar ready with the net.'

Erik and Ivar spread out one of the nets between them and with those carrying spears pointed towards the beast they advanced upon it. The creature stood and gazed balefully at the men. To their good fortune it made no move apart from blowing flame in their direction.

'Now,' cried Odo.

Erik and Ivar threw the net over the beast. It was weighted with lead weights and completely engulfed the monster who gave a great cry and with its curved talons began to tear great rents in the net.

'Spears quickly,' shouted Odo.

The men with spears ran forward and drove them into the beast. This just served to enrage the animal which redoubled its effort to be rid of the net. The contest was ended when Arni stepped forward and with one mighty blow from his double headed war axe cleaved the head from the beast's body. The creature shuddered and collapsed onto the floor of the cavern.

'Well done men,' said Odo, as they gathered around the creature to retrieve the net and their spears.

'Methinks that was just a baby,' remarked Arni. 'Thor help us when we encounter its larger relatives!'

'We need to find the lair of the witch,' said Odo. 'There must be another cavern and the passage from which this creature emerged is the one we will follow.'

The men entered the passageway and cautiously moved along it. One of the men marked their progress with regular cuts in the limestone. They had no idea how many passageways there were and getting lost in what could be a labyrinth of caves and connecting pathways was scary enough.

On several occasions they were met with a choice of tunnels to follow. The decision was made by the footprints they could see on the sandy floor. The passageway with the most footprints was the one they followed.

After what seemed an eternity the band emerged into a cavern twice the size of the first one they had encountered. Huge stalagmites dotted the floor and this afforded the men good cover. At the centre of the cavern was a rock pool whose surface reflected the light from many braziers set in stands on the far most side. Three wooden stakes covered in dried blood were set in the floor. A table of rough-hewn oak was situated close by the stakes.

A noise behind the men caused them all to draw their weapons and spin round. They relaxed when they saw it was one of the men Odo had detailed to explore the right hand passage leading away from the first cavern.

'It is as you had suggested my lord,' the man whispered.

'Good,' grunted Odo quietly.

Just as he finished speaking, the well-muscled man wearing the helmet of stag horns entered the cavern from the far side. He led three women behind him tied together by rope. One of the women was the lady Nevena. One of the minstrels playing the pipes had accompanied him. The man with the helmet of stag horns untied the women and secured each of them to a separate stake. His final act was to draw a wickedly sharp looking knife and advance upon each in turn. Odo stiffened and it was all he could do to prevent himself leaping forward to slay the man and rescue the women. But Arni held him back in a vice like grip.

The man with the knife cut the white shifts away from each of the women so they stood bound and naked at their stakes. Two of them were wailing inconsolably. Only the lady Nevena stood quietly, tall and proud at her stake.

The minstrel and the man with the head gear then withdrew from the cavern. For several seconds nothing happened. Then the prince of the Dumnonii entered the cavern. He stopped, held his arms aloft and cried out loud.

'Gwrtheyrna, oh wise one, priestess to the Dumnonii, take these as gifts from my humble self for you to sacrifice and to bring good fortune on my household, my people and our crops.'

He uttered many other invocations in a language that Odo and his men could not understand. Finally, he prostrated himself on the sandy floor and crawled backwards out of the cavern.

Silence descended.

Though it was cold in the huge grotto, every one of Odo's men was sweating. They watched as a mist formed on the waters of the pool in front of them. The mist rose and became a dense fog so that they lost sight of the captives bound at the stakes on the other side.

The silence was split with a deafening roar and heavy rasping. This increased the men's tension. As the fog began to disperse they could see two huge beasts, exact replicas of the one they had slain. These were at least twenty feet tall standing on two legs with leathery looking bodies, snake-like heads and necks with huge curled horns and legs that bore wicked looking curved-talons.

They stood either side of the women bound at the stakes and breathed fire into the air.

The men then witnessed a miracle. The still waters of the pond boiled up and a creature arose out of the water and seemed to walk upon its surface until it reached the sandy floor of the far side of the cavern.

'Easy my beauties, now is not the time,' uttered a voice that was strangely young and warm sounding. The sorceress had arrived dripping water off animal fleeces that adorned her body.

One of the women at the stakes had passed out through fear. The other kept up a high pitched wailing. Only the lady Nevena kept a watchful silence.

'I see the gods have been kind to me,' said the witch looking at the lady Nevena. 'A high born lady who seems not afraid. How I have waited for one like you to sacrifice.'

The hag, for by this time the men could see she was very old, advanced upon her victims crooning softly to herself. She looked upon each in turn before turning to the table where she laid out various items. The man with the helmet of stag horns had reappeared and stood waiting for instructions.

Odo turned to the man who carried the bow. He was their best archer.

'Rollo, the witch is yours,' he whispered.

Rollo drew an arrow from his quiver placed it on his bow and took careful aim. He drew the string back, quivering slightly from the effort, and prayed to Skadi, goddess of hunting, for his aim. Then two things happened.

The first was that Rollo released his goose feathered shaft. The second was that simultaneously, as the arrow left the bow, the sorceress turned extending her left arm directly toward Rollo. The arrow, which had been aimed accurately at her back, altered its course upwards and passed harmlessly over her head. Rollo frantically reached for another arrow in his quiver but found himself seemingly paralysed. He could not move his arms; they appeared to be held by some unseen force.

Odo, realising the gravity of the situation, took half his men left around the pool and launched a spear at the surprised man in the helmet of stag horns. The spear took him in the chest and he collapsed to the floor. One of the men accompanying Odo cast another spear in the witch's direction. This deflected her attention from Rollo, who released from his invisible restraint, leapt behind a huge stalagmite where Arni took him by the arm and indicated he should follow him and the remaining men.

Odo and his men attempted to rush the sorceress but the nearest beast, which had been virtually motionless to this point, began to howl and expel huge gouts of fire in their direction. This checked them. The other creature took two bounds towards them and added its howling and venom to its mate. Odo and his men could not move forward. They had to stay out of range of the creature's fire or risk being severely burnt and maimed.

'Shout lads and wave your weapons. We need to keep the hag distracted,' said Odo, knowing that Arni had taken the rest of the men around the right hand side of the pool. Hopefully, he was in position behind the creatures and their mistress ready to join the fray with the element of surprise on his side.

'Siegfried was with Arni's men. As he followed him he tugged at Arni's arm.

'Not now boy,' said Arni shrugging him off.

'Lord, lord, the only way to kill the aglaecwif, the she monster, is to use a wooden stake through her heart.'

Arni hesitated. 'How do you know this boy?'

'An old hunter from our village told me,' replied Siegfried.

'Lars, give me your spear,' commanded Arni. On

taking hold of the spear he took the end between his massive hands and snapped off the wicked looking iron barb.

'You'd better be right boy.'

With that, Arni and his men rounded the last big stalagmite and rushed at the woman. The witch sensed their presence and began to turn. She swung her left hand in their direction and shouted a curse. It was if they had run into an invisible wall.

Odo, seeing their plight, took an axe from the man next to him and threw it at the old lady. Her senses detected the flight of the axe and she turned to pluck it out of the air with both hands. This distraction caused the spell she had cast on Arni's men to be broken. Arni leapt forward and with a mighty roar cast his ash spear, minus its iron head, at the back of the woman. His enormous strength gave the spear vital impetus; its natural flight having been severely affected by the removal of its weighted iron head. The end of the wooden shaft entered the old crone's back. Such was the force that Arni had thrown the spear with that the end protruded out from the front of the witch. The gods alone knew whether it had penetrated her heart.

The old woman gave a loud shriek, staggered and plunged into the pool to vanish out of sight. The waters boiled up and a thick mist began to arise from the surface of the water.

The two massive beasts began to roar in unison and advance upon the men.

'Arni, have one of the men cut the women free and get over here. We'll have to distract these beasts,' shouted Odo.

Arni turned to Siegfried. 'Siegfried, you heard our lord, I'm relying on you to free the women; quickly now.'

Siegfried took his knife out from its sheath and darted towards the posts. Arni and his men ran to join Odo where they did their best to howl insults at the beasts and engage their attention, staying out of range of their thunderbolts of flame.

Without their mistress the beasts seemed at a loss as to what to do other than focus their wrath at the group of men who had invaded their lair.

The unexpected noise and commotion in the cavern had an unexpected side effect. It had drawn the prince and his household warriors back to the cave. They spilled out of one of the passageways.

'Just what we need to compound our difficulties,' shouted Arni to Odo.

But the gods smiled upon Odo and his men. One of the beasts seeing the prince and his men took them for more intruders and turned its attention upon them. It advanced upon them shooting flames in their direction. They immediately retreated back into the passageway from which they had come and remained bottled up there as the creature advanced upon the opening.

Siegfried, without any immediate threat, cut the bonds of all three women and with the help of the lady Nevena, who had remained calm throughout the ordeal, dragged the other two weeping women back around the pond in the direction from which they had come.

Using his initiative, and not waiting for Odo and the rest of the men, he followed the cut marks in the limestone back up the passageway they had come along.

Odo, seeing Siegfried vanish up the corridor of limestone, shouted at his men to disengage. The men needed no second invitation and retreated after Siegfried.

The band of men pounded up the tunnel. They followed the cut marks in the limestone until they reached the first cavern they had encountered. Instead of following the original corridor, Odo guided them down the tunnel he had sent the two men with the rope. It emerged into a much smaller cavern that had another passageway leaving it almost opposite the one they had come down.

Odo directed all the men bar Arni and two others to follow that tunnel. Arni looked enquiringly at Odo.

'We need to buy some time,' said Odo. 'One of those creatures will be following.'

As if on cue, a burst of flame issued from the tunnel which they had just come down.

The two men who had remained with Odo carried the last of the weighted nets they had brought. Fortunately, the tunnel entrance was narrow and low in height.

‘Quickly now,’ commanded Odo.

The two men knew what to do. They held the net up over the passage’s entrance. The creature propelled itself straight into it. The men couldn’t hold the net and were forced to let it go. But it had the desired effect. The creature was enmeshed in the folds of the net and came to a standstill while it howled and tore at its folds with its wickedly curved talons.

Both Odo and Arni sprang forward. Odo thrust at the creature with the last remaining spear and Arni flailed at the creature with his huge axe. Odo shouted at the two remaining men to leave quickly.

Arni, unable to reach the creature’s head concentrated on its legs. With one mighty swipe of his axe he severed one of its legs in two. The creature howled in pain and lurched to one side. Odo drew his sword, Dragon Slayer, and brought it down upon its other leg. His sword didn’t carry the weight, or power, of Arni’s axe but the creature was now severely disabled.

‘Enough,’ cried Odo, ‘time to go.’

Both Odo and Arni ran down the opposite tunnel.

Rollo, the bowman, was waiting for them at the tunnel's end. Its end, as Odo had hoped, gave out onto the cove where Thorvald, their ship and the rest of the crew were waiting. A rope, attached around an axe head driven deep into the limestone floor, dangled down the side of the cliff onto the beach.

'Quick my lord, I'll keep the monster at bay,' said Rollo notching an arrow to his bow.

Arni grabbed the rope and slid rapidly down it onto the beach followed closely by Odo. They burnt their hands, but that was a small price to pay.

Once Odo and Arni had gone, and with no sign of the monster, Rollo shouldered his bow and swung himself out over the ledge and slid down the rope.

Having made the beach the three headed for Skidbladnir which Thorvald and the remaining men had launched into the sea. Fortunately, it was a calm night and the sea was still.

As the men boarded the ship a huge explosion of flame issued out of the tunnel opening in the cliff above, followed by a crash. The creature had jumped onto the beach.

Thorvald issued the command to row. 'Pull men, pull, we need to be out of here and fast.'

The Vikings put their backs into their rowing and the slim craft shot away from the beach.

The monster which had followed them lay dying on the sand. Its remaining leg had finally given way and it was bleeding to death.

As the men rowed hard out to sea, Odo walked to the front of the ship to where the three women sat. Siegfried had found cloaks to cover the women. The lady Nevena stood as Odo approached.

'Your ordeal is now over my lady. We will soon have you reunited with your people.'

'I thank you, my lord, for rescuing me and these poor ladies here.'

'You were very brave and calm my lady, astonishingly so given the horrors facing you.'

'I knew you would come,' the lady Nevena replied, 'that helped calm me. Once I saw Siegfried in the village I knew you could not be far away.'

'Ah yes, brave lad is Siegfried. He will make a good Viking.'

'He is brave,' she said turning to where Siegfried squatted on the deck looking embarrassed.

'What will happen to us lord?' asked one of the other two women.

'That depends on the lord Cadeyrn,' said Odo, 'one thing is for certain, you cannot return to the Dumnonii.' The woman went silent.

'Get some rest and I'll speak with you in the morning,'said Odo turning to walk back towards the rear of their vessel.

As he walked back up the craft he leant down and touched the men on the shoulder who had been with him through their exploit in the caves, thanking them for their endeavours.

'I wouldn't want to go through that again,' said Arni when he reached the stern. 'I hope that witch can't touch us out here.'

'Let's put our trust in Odin and Aegir, god of the sea,' replied Odo. 'The gods know, we should have delighted them with that adventure.'

'What are your orders, my lord?' asked Agnar the helmsman.

'We sail North East. It's a clear night so let's keep the coast in sight on our port bow.'

As they cleared the cove a light wind sprang up from the South West and Arni ordered the men to raise the sail. The Vikings shipped their oars and their ship moved swiftly and silently through the waters, the bow wave iridescent in the moon light.

Siegfried and the Vikings - 'The Dragon's Breath'

Chapter Twenty Two

The Viking ship sailed through the night and dawn brightened clear and sunny.

'It's going to another warm day,' grumbled Arni.

'Better that than the ice and snow of the fjords,' replied Odo.

'Unlike you, I miss the cold and the ice,' said Arni.

'Agnar, take us inshore. We need to eat, rest and the ladies would no doubt like to stretch their legs,' ordered Odo.

'Aye, my lord,' replied Agnar, swinging the steering oar hard to starboard. The ship surged towards the coast line.

Agnar drove the craft onto a shingle beach and men leaped out to secure the vessel. A number of men headed for the bluffs above the beach to scout out their surroundings.

Bodvar soon had a fire going and was cooking up a simple stew of rabbit and onions into which he threw some herbs. The smell was appetising and Siegfried, for one, couldn't wait to eat his share.

The three ladies under the protection of two of Odo's men walked along the beach until they found a pool of clear water in which they could wash.

Odo, Arni, Thorvald and Ingvar were sitting on the shingle near the fire.

'Brother, the gods must favour you. That was a dangerous mission we could have avoided,' said Ingvar.

'We were oath bound to attempt the rescue of the lady Nevena,' replied Odo.

'Since when do we bind ourselves to other men?' asked Ingvar.

'When I say we must and when the men agree,' said Odo.

'Your liking for the lady Nevena is obvious and clouds your judgement.'

'We rescued the lady, killed the witch, slaughtered two of the creatures, and we are here alive and kicking, so what's your problem?' said Arni menacingly.

'I fear we are not out of the woods yet,' said Ingvar.

'You should have been named Ingvar the pessimist,'

said Arni. But Ingvar was to be proved right.

As the men were eating their fill of Bodvar's stew, the men who had been keeping watch above the shoreline were seen running back to the beach.

'My lord, armed horsemen, at least thirty heading this way,' said Hakon, one of the scouts.

Odo issued the command for everyone to board Skidblabnir.

The men who had not finished eating had to tip the remains of their stew onto the beach.

'Just my luck,' grumbled Hakon to his friend Hastein, 'I'm starving and was looking forward to some of that. I've had enough of hard bread and stale cheese.'

'Better that than a Celtic spear in your guts,' replied Hastein smiling.

The men quickly gathered up their things and boarded the ship and those remaining on the shore pushed the craft back into the sea. As the ship floated off the beach they scrambled on board. The men at the oars pulled hard and they were just out of spear range when the horsemen galloped onto the beach. The shingle slowed down their already tired horses enabling the Vikings to be some distance from the shore before the band of warriors pulled up at the sea's edge and cast spears in their direction. They all fell short.

'Dumonii,' said Seisal who had sharp eyesight.

'They got here quicker than I expected,' said Odo.

Agnar took the ship well out to sea before turning North East to follow the coastline. Arni ordered the sail to be raised as the wind was freshening.

Odo looked hard at the coast and thought he could see sunlight glinting off spear heads and chain mail.

'They're tracking us my lord,' said Arni.

'I know,' said Odo, 'let's see if they tire of their pursuit.'

As time passed Odo and his men could still see the horsemen following them along the coast line.

'Agnar, head due South until we can no longer be seen from the shore,' ordered Odo.

The longship moved swiftly along its new course and the shoreline receded rapidly from view.

They were well out of sight of land before Odo

requested Agnar to resume their original course.

'That should give them cause to think,' said Odo to Thorvald and Arni.

'I doubt it, said Thorvald, 'they know we are headed for the lands of the Regni. I fear we have not seen the last of them yet and we will have the Durotriges to contend with. I fear the prince of the Dumnonii set them on us and will do so again.'

Odo went silent for many moments.

'Agnar,' called Odo, 'set a course for Gaul.'

The men sat at their ease along the craft and Siegfried, for one, was enjoying the motion of the ship as it surged through the waters towards Gaul under the power of its single sail. The sky was blue with few clouds slowly passing overhead. He had never left the mainland of Britain and was excited at the prospect of seeing a foreign land. He knew that that the Celts of Gaul were closely related to his kind and he was keen to see how life was lived across the sea to the south. He revelled in being with these hard, capable, but mainly kind, men who had adopted him. This was far more exciting than living in his village carrying out the daily chores and learning about farming, though he felt a trace of guilt at having deserted his family.

It was early evening when land was spotted off their starboard bow. The men said it was a small island; the name of which they did not know. Gaul was just beyond and it appeared that Odo seemed keen to make the coast of the mainland before nightfall. A large headland appeared but Agnar deliberately altered course to the East. He did not like the look of the promontory that stretched out into the sea; fearing vicious outcrops of rock that would gut their ship.

A long strip of sandy beach came into view protected on both sides by rocky peninsulas and it was towards this that Agnar steered their vessel driving it hard up onto the sand. A number of men jumped overboard and headed for the ridge above the shore to scout out their surroundings. Siegfried was asked to help Bodvar search for driftwood to light a fire.

After a night and day of sailing, despite the brief respite on the beach in Britain, the men were looking forward to a night's sleep. The evening was warm and balmy. The fire was only needed to cook with.

The Vikings appeared to have the beach to themselves. There was no sign of the local inhabitants, no fishing boats drawn up on the sand, no goats even. This was strange as Osric knew there was an ancient fortified settlement on a hilltop about a mile to the south.

The following morning Odo organised a group of fifteen men to accompany him to the fortified settlement Osric knew. They could do with more flour for bread, cheese and meat. Odo expected no trouble as they had no enemies here, though the men went armed with shields slung across their backs. Thorvald, as usual, was left in command of the ship on the beach. Osric, Arni, Ingvar, Siegfried and Karl were among those chosen to accompany Odo.

It was warmer here than in Britain and the men were soon sweating under their leather jerkins and mail brynjas that some of them chose to wear.

Four of the men were sent on ahead in pairs as scouts

to ensure that the remaining twelve were not surprised in any way.

The Viking band climbed steadily upwards away from the beach towards a low escarpment they could see in the distance. The countryside was undulating and heavy with copses of trees. Where the land was open, thick, tall grass grew.

Many trees had been felled for their wood and cultivated plots thick with barley were nestled in the bottoms of the small valleys they walked through. The smell of elderflower hung heavy in the air and early black berries covered the brambles at the edges of the copses. Siegfried and Karl were busy picking and eating them as they walked.

'This is beautiful country' said Siegfried to Karl, 'and these black berries are sweet.'

'They are,' replied Karl, 'but it's strange that there is no-one around. Not even a cow.'

The men halted at the foot of the escarpment and awaited the return of the scouts who had fanned out either side of the settlement Osric told them was situated on its top. The men soon returned.

'No sign of life,' said Lars, one of two men who had gone east around the settlement.

'Nothing moving on the west side either,' said Lief who had been part of the other pair.

'Let's see what awaits us then,' said Odo, moving purposefully uphill.

As they breasted the escarpment, a palisade of wood greeted them. It was built on top of an earthen wall and surrounded a large cluster of round thatched huts whose tops could be seen above the palisade's wall. A large rectangular hall dominated the centre of the settlement. Nothing moved, not even a bird.

'A prosperous looking place but it has the smell of death about it,' remarked Arni.

The main entrance to the settlement was situated on the eastern approach and the heavy wooden gates were open. Nothing stirred.

'Let's close up,' commanded Odo, drawing his sword dragon slayer and slipping his left arm through the leather thongs of his shield. The rest of the men did likewise.

In two rows with shields on their arms, and Siegfried and Karl following behind, the men approached the gate. They stopped ten paces from the entrance. Odo called out then called out again. Nothing stirred. Not even a dog barked.

'Let's enter,' said Odo as the men passed through the gate and spilled out onto an area of beaten earth that served as the entrance way into the settlement. The place was completely still.

'Siegfried, you and Karl wait here and shout if anyone approaches from the outside. The rest of you follow me.'

The men split into two groups under Odo's and Arni's leadership and set off to explore the settlement. It didn't take them long.

There was no-one there.

No dogs, no chickens. The only things alive that could be seen were rats which scuttled away when the men approached.

The main hall appeared as if a meal had been in progress. Wooden platters containing the remains of food were on the tables though rats had been busy harvesting what they could. Wooden goblets contained liquid which clearly wasn't mead but a wine of some sort.

A rotting haunch of pig was suspended on an iron gantry above a fire long since burnt out.

The same was to be found in the thatched huts of the villagers. It was as if the inhabitants had suddenly vanished into thin air. There was no sign of crisis or conflict. No blood on the ground, no weapons to be seen apart from those hung on walls or contained in chests that belonged to the wealthier villagers.

The men, who had gathered in the main square, muttered quietly and touched their amulets. There was evil in the air and nothing to explain what had happened.

A shout from the gate roused the men from their torpor. Siegfried ran breathlessly into the square.

'Men my lord, twenty at least,' he said. Of Karl there was no sign.

Before they could react, the unknown men marched

in through the gate and surrounded Odo and his men. They were well armed and looked as if they knew their business.

A broad, bearded, red headed man walked forward.

'And who may you be?' he enquired calmly.

Odo explained who they were and what they were doing there.

'You have come at a bad time,' said red beard. 'There is an evil spirit at work here that has blighted our people and our land. This is the second of our settlements that has suffered this fate. We do not understand what has caused this. My advisers tell me that this is the work of pirates and that our folk have been taken into captivity and sold as slaves; men such as yourself maybe?'

Odo ignored the insinuation and asked who red beard was.

'I am Calliges, a prince of the Redones, and this land is mine.'

'Calliges, I can assure you that this is not the work of my men. As I said, we are looking to buy supplies before we continue our journey. There is no sign of struggle here and I cannot imagine the inhabitants of this settlement went easily without a fight.'

'That may be,' replied Calliges. 'In the mean time you will surrender your weapons to me.'

'I am not an enemy Calliges and we do not surrender our weapons lightly,' replied Odo.

Calliges took a moment to assess the well armed and capable looking men in front of him and reached a decision.

'Keep your weapons but I ask that you come with us to our camp which is not far from here.'

Odo had no choice but to comply, outnumbered and surrounded as they were by Calliges' men.

Calliges led them to a loosely fortified encampment a mile south of the village. Odo discerned a further ten warriors and a gaggle of slaves and serving women at the encampment, where he and his men were invited to sit on large colourful woollen blankets whilst the serving women brought them watered wine in wooden goblets.

Calliges opened the discussion by asking who they were and where they were from. Odo replied and described what had brought them to Gaul.

'I have heard of Odo the dragon slayer,' said Calliges. 'I have relatives amongst the Morini who have told me of your exploits. I welcome you and your men to our humble camp and look forward to hearing how you slayed the monsters in Britain later this evening when we dine on wild boar that we slew yesterday.'

Before Odo could reply, one of Calliges' men ran into the camp and spoke urgently to Calliges in a dialect Odo and his men could not understand.

Calliges looked at Odo speculatively.

'It seems armed men are headed this way my lord Odo. Would they be the rest of your crew? If not, we may have a fight on our hands.'

Odo, impressed by Calliges' calmness, agreed that in all likelihood they were.

As the men rose to their feet, Thorvald and some fifteen of the Viking band approached the camp in a line with swords drawn and shields overlapping.

'They are my men,' said Odo. He called out to Thorvald, and those accompanying him, to lower their weapons and join them.

At the approach of the Redones back at the settlement, Siegfried and Karl agreed that Karl should race back to Thorvald and warn him of their presence.

Thorvald had wasted no time in reacting, bringing the bulk of the men with him leaving a handful under Agnar with their ship.

The lady Nevena had also accompanied Thorvald and now walked into the centre of the camp. She addressed Calliges directly, explaining who she was.

'We are honoured,' said Calliges smiling broadly, 'it's not every day we can extend courtesy to a princess of the Regni. But what, may I ask, is a princess of the Regni doing amongst these barbarians?'

Odo bristled at this description, but if the lady Nevena was offended she didn't show it. She walked across to Odo, rested her hand on his arm and explained briefly how she came to be with them and that she owed them her life.

'This will truly be a tale we will enjoy hearing later when we dine,' replied Calliges. 'But first I would ask the lord Odo to accompany me to another one of my settlements, not far from here.'

Odo, Arni, the lady Nevena and a couple of the Viking band accompanied Calliges and five of his men to a fortified settlement to the west of where they were camped.

The site that greeted them was similar to the one they had encountered earlier. The place was abandoned with no sign of struggle. The villagers and animals had seemingly disappeared into thin air.

'This is a puzzle that is beyond my learning and understanding,' commented the lady Nevena to Odo and Calliges.

'A puzzle indeed,' replied Calliges, 'and one that I would ask Odo, the dragon slayer, to solve. In return you would earn the gratitude of the Redones and a handsome sum of gold.'

'I would very much like to help,' said Odo, 'but I have a duty to return the lady Nevena safely to her brother and complete my undertaking to him.'

Calliges studied Odo for several seconds and smiled.

'Let me see if I can persuade you over dinner,' he said turning away to begin the trek back to his encampment.

Dinner was a simple affair with plates of wild boar and onions served with a raw red wine that the Vikings winced at when first tasted. But it went well with the meat and soon the men were relaxed and exchanging war stories around a blazing fire.

Odo recounted his adventures in Britain which impressed the listening Redones. Siegfried came in for some praise which embarrassed him. Following the recounting of their exploits Calliges turned to Odo.

'My lord, it would seem to me that you have earned a reputation for helping humble folk like ourselves rid themselves of evil and evil is at work here among my people. I know not what is the cause of our missing brethren but I feel sure you are the man who could find out. This would be a worthy challenge in your quest for redemption.'

Nevena, who had been listening to the exchange, spoke up.

'My lord Odo, I am in no rush to return to my brother.

I beseech you to help Calliges solve this mystery,' she said looking at him imploringly.

Odo's resolve melted away.

'We will do all we can to help,' he replied.

The following morning Odo sat in counsel with Calliges.

'How many other settlements are there in the vicinity? We need to find a pattern here that may help us find out what is happening to your people.'

Calliges drew a map of the area in the earth at his feet.

'So, two settlements have been attacked so far and both close to the coast. There has been no trouble further inland?' asked Odo.

'No, just these two settlements,' replied Calliges.

'Is there anything else you can tell me? When, for example, did these incidents take place?'

Calliges thought hard for several moments.

'Only that they both occurred on the night of a full moon and a high tide,' he said.

'Looking at your map, there is only one other of your

settlements that lies close to the coast and that is to the North of here. And it's a full moon in three days time. That is where we shall go,' Odo said.

'Very well, we will accompany you there,' said Calliges.

'My lord, no offence, but I would prefer it if my men and I undertook this reconnaissance on our own.'

'So be it, but to avoid any hostilities I will send one of my men with you. He is a renowned warrior and has relatives in the settlement.'

'Very well,' replied Odo.

Odo gathered his men around him and selected fifteen to accompany him. He asked Thorvald to return to Skidbladnir with the rest.

'Uncle, I need you to bring the ship around the headland and moor in the bay that lies below where we are going. We shall then set up a relay of messengers between us so we are both kept informed as to progress. I don't know whether this evil emanates from the sea, whether it is the work of pirates, monsters or something more sinister but I need you to keep a wary eye out for all possibilities.'

Thorvald nodded.

The name of the warrior of the Redones was Teutorix, a slim, effeminate looking young man with long fair hair tied in two braids down his back. Unusually, he carried two swords strapped across his back, no shield or spear.

Siegfried found himself walking next to Teutorix at the head of the small column making its way to the village in question. He was fascinated by the young man's swords.

'You carry no shield or spear?' asked Siegfried.

'No, boy, my swords are enough,' he replied.

'You fight with both at once?' asked Siegfried.

'That I do. I am a Dymacherus and learnt my trade from a Greek mercenary who my father employed as a body guard. It is a noble way to fight though not without danger. Very few men can handle two swords with skill.'

'Will you show me?'

'I only draw my swords in anger,' laughed Teutorix, 'but should the occasion arise I will.'

The band of men reached the settlement in the early

afternoon and Teutorix went ahead to explain the presence of the strangers.

Once inside the fortified village Odo and Arni had a good look around.

'All seems normal here my lord,' remarked Arni.

'It does, but if this evil is to strike again I warrant it will be here and maybe soon,' said Odo.

The first night passed without incident as did the next.

By the beginning of the third day some of the men were getting fractious through the inactivity, notably Ingvar.

'Brother, this is a waste of time. Let's relieve the head man of a small amount of his silver as payment for our trouble, return the lady Nevena to her tribe, collect the gold that is owed us and seek pastures new.'

'Ever impatient Ingvar, don't be, for this evil will strike here soon enough,' said Odo.

'Hah! How do you know?' asked Ingvar.

'This evil strikes on a full moon and it's a full moon tonight, along with a high tide,' said Odo.

‘I’ll believe that when it happens,’ responded Ingvar turning away.

To relieve the tedium Odo arranged for the men to practice their sword and shield drills in mock fights between themselves. He left them to it and accompanied by Arni set off to explore the countryside outside the village.

Within an hour the men had worked up a fair sweat. Teutorix and a number of the local men had watched the exercises with interest.

Ingvar turned to Rolf.

‘This is getting boring. Why don’t we see what the local warriors have in the way of skills, particularly pretty boy over there?’

Rolf agreed, only too keen to keen to seek a distraction and please his lord. He ambled over to Teutorix.

‘Can you use those things, or are they just adorning you to make you look pretty?’ asked Rolf pointing at the swords on Teutorix’s back.

‘Better you don’t find out,’ replied Teutorix looking

steadily at Rolf.

'Is that a challenge? I hear a challenge,' cried Rolf.

'No challenge, of that I can assure you,' replied Teutorix.

'Are you a coward?' asked Rolf.

Teutorix just gazed at Rolf steadily.

Having made the provocation, and with Ingvar and the rest of Vikings, including Siegfried, now watching him, Rolf felt he had to see it through.

'Come on pretty boy let's see what you are made of,' said Rolf drawing his sword and hefting his shield on his left arm.

Teutorix made no move, which irritated Rolf.

Rolf advanced towards Teutorix and tapped his arms with the flat of his sword. Teutorix stood perfectly still.

Rolf was now beginning to feel a fool. He jabbed the point of his sword hard into the leather jerkin that covered the chest of Teutorix before bringing the flat of his blade in a wide arc into his upper arm. The blows must have hurt but Teutorix didn't flinch.

Rolf began to repeat the moves with more intent. As

he jabbed forward, Teutorix moved sideways to his right like lightning. Rolf heard the metallic rasp of two swords and felt one of them strike him on his upper arm with a numbing blow. As he began to turn to his right, the other lashed down onto his right hand making him let go of his sword. He turned to face Teutorix with just his shield between them. Both swords were a blur in front of him. One feinted low, the other high. Rolf couldn't move his shield quickly enough to ward off the blows. Teutorix danced from side to side keeping his swords high, pointed towards him.

Rolf was an experienced warrior and knew that attack was often the best form of defence and a shield is a capable weapon if used properly. He charged towards Teutorix intending to bludgeon him with his shield before driving its rim up under his chin.

Teutorix knew what was coming, rode the shield charge then dropped sideways to his knees and brought the flat sides of both swords up hard into Rolf's unprotected groin.

Rolf howled, dropped his shield and sank to the

ground, curled into a ball clutching himself with both hands. He was in great pain though not seriously injured. The rest of the Vikings burst out laughing. Even Ingvar was impressed.

'You move and fight well for a pretty boy, said Ingvar.

'Do you want to find out how well I fight?' said Teutorix.

'No, no, that was a display worthy of a great warrior,' said Ingvar quickly before dropping down beside Rolf to tend to him.

At that moment Odo and Arni strode back into the settlement. Odo was not pleased at what had taken place and offered his apologies to Teutorix.

'No apology required,' said Teutorix, 'it was just harmless fun.'

Odo dispersed the watching Vikings and organised them into patrols to scout the nearby country side including the coast.

'Do you think they will find something?' asked Arni.

'No, but it will keep them occupied for the rest of the day and out of trouble,' replied Odo.

The day wore on and early evening saw the return of the Vikings to the settlement. In their absence Odo had been thinking hard about his plans for the evening. Thorvald had arrived and he, Arni and Odo sat to discuss the outcome of that thinking.

He had asked Teutorix to explain to the villagers that they needed to vacate the settlement but that this must be done stealthily and only when dusk came. They were to leave everything behind and seek shelter overnight in the dense woodland that cloaked the nearby slopes.

'If the demon strikes tonight, which my instincts tell me will be the case, then I want none of us to be inside the village,' said Odo, 'we will surround the settlement in pairs and keep a sharp lookout.'

The Vikings ate their evening meal but no wine was allowed as Odo wanted his men to remain sharp for what may come. He explained his plans and as dusk fell the men left the settlement along with the villagers and went to their appointed positions.

It was a warm and cloudless night with the full moon bathing the landscape in a soft white light.

As the moon reached its zenith a mist descended on the settlement and visibility was severely reduced.

'By Odin's breath, this feels unnatural and makes things difficult to see,' said Arni quietly to Odo.

'It does, and I fear the terror will strike soon,' replied Odo.

Not many minutes later a slithering sound could

be heard; not just one isolated sound but several. Odo and Arni cocked their ears and looked hard through the mist. They were positioned closest to the entrance to the settlement hunkered down behind a small stand of oak trees. They could just about make out the gate which had been left open and what they saw were demons the like of which they had never seen before approaching the flat ground in front of the gate.

There were three of them. Long snakelike beings with bodies the size of mature oak trees. The nearest beast appeared to have three heads. A yellowish vapour issued from its reptilian mouths.

Two goats had been tethered just outside the gate and they began to bleat alarmingly. This had been Odo's idea.

One of the snakelike demons advanced upon the goats and spewed out a stream of fiery yellow vapour which engulfed the nearest animal. The poor creature seemingly vanished into thin air. The other goat was similarly dispatched.

'By Odin's hairy arse, look at that!' exclaimed Arni.

'Quiet,' hissed Odo, 'we don't want to attract their attention.'

The three demons slithered into the fortified village looking for more prey. Once out of sight Odo rose up.

'Arni, quick, help me secure the gates.' Odo advanced quickly towards them summoning the two other Vikings who had been keeping watch some thirty yards away.

Between the four of them they manhandled the gates closed. Odo turned to address one of the men as quietly as he could.

'Ivar, we need some stout stakes. Find the next pair of men and cut down the first saplings you can find.'

Ivar and his fellow Viking departed quickly.

'These gates are fine to keep marauders out but

weren't designed to keep people in never mind demons,' said Odo quietly. 'Let's retreat to the oak trees over there. I don't fancy following the fate of the goats just yet.'

Ivar and his three companions eventually returned with four thick pointed stakes. Between them and with the help of Odo and Arni they thrust them into the ground as far as they would go and wedged them against the gates.

'Let's see if that contains them,' whispered Odo as they retreated back to the stand of oak trees.

'We need to inform the others,' said Odo turning to the four Vikings. 'Split up and carry the word of what happened here. Ivar get back to the ship and ask Thorvald to keep an eye out. These creatures must come from the sea.' The men departed.

No sooner had the men gone than a high pitched shrieking filled the air. The demons had returned to the gate to find their way out had been barred. One of the beasts swung its tail viciously at the gates in an attempt to break them open but the wooden stakes were serving their purpose.

After several attempts the demons went quiet.

The mist hung over the ground and Odo and Arni watched anxiously. Siegfried arrived at that moment.

'My lord, Thorvald has been informed and awaits your instructions.'

Before Odo could reply a fiery glow lit up the mist and before their eyes the gates vanished in a cloud of yellow vapour. The three angry monsters slithered out of the settlement their heads probing in all directions.

'Back, back behind these trees,' whispered Odo urgently. Siegfried and Arni needed no second bidding.

Seeing nothing immediately around them the demons slithered off in the direction of the sea.

Odo, Arni and Siegfried followed at a safe distance. While they were hidden by the mist they didn't need to close the gap as they could clearly make out their tracks. The three demons made for the beach and plunged into the surf. The sea and the mist swallowed them up as the three arrived at the water's edge.

'At least we now know what is causing the

disappearance of the local folk here,' remarked Odo.

'But how do we defeat them when with one breath they can make you disappear? This is the work of great evil,' replied Arni touching his amulet, a small bronze replica of Thor's hammer.

They returned to the settlement and the anxious gaze of several of the Vikings who had assembled by the gates. Odo brought them up to date with what had happened and then commanded that they seek sleep within the settlement with a guard posted throughout the night.

As Odo turned away, he saw Siegfried standing before him clutching something in his hand.

'What is it lad?'

'My lord, I found this and others like it by the gate, the gate which the demons destroyed.' Siegfried held out a sliver of metal.

Odo took it and, with Arni beside him, looked more closely at it in the light of the full moon.

'A nail,' Arni remarked, 'and unless I'm mistaken it's made of lead.'

They returned to examine the ground around where the gate had stood and saw several more nails that lay on the ground.

'So, it seems not everything can be destroyed by the demons breath,' remarked Odo.

'Well done Siegfried, this could be significant. But, for now let's turn in and we'll look at this again in the morning.'

Chapter Twenty Three

As the sun rose above the horizon the Vikings made breakfast. Odo, Arni, Thorvald and Ingvar sat around in a circle looking at the lead nails Odo held in his hands. Thorvald was the first to speak.

'It seems to me that we could cover a shield with thinly beaten lead and that might let us get close enough to one of the demons to kill it.'

'It would have to be a big shield uncle, if the bearer of it is not to be touched by that foul breath,' said Ingvar.

'Maybe we could cover a helmet and leggings too,' replied Thorvald.

'That sounds very risky to me,' replied Ingvar.

'Distraction, that's all we need,' said Thorvald, 'then one or two us could come from behind with our spears and swords and see to the beast.'

'Assuming we can deal with them one at a time,' shot back Ingvar, 'and we would need to entice them back onto land. I cannot see how we can tackle them in the sea. Our ship would be damaged by one yellow breath.'

'Lead is the answer,' said Odo, 'but we need to think

how best to employ its use. And, you are right, Ingvar, we do not know where their lair is, and we cannot risk Skidbladnir.'

While they were discussing the subject, the villagers returned and Teutorix approached them. Odo invited him to join them and brought him up to date with what had happened during the night.

'We need your smith to fashion lead coverings for shields, helmets with face visors and leggings for two of us,' said Odo, 'can he do that?'

'Yes, my lord. It will take all the supplies of lead we have and maybe more,' replied Teutorix.

'Can the extra lead be stripped from buildings and fences in the settlement?' asked Odo.

'I'll see what can be done lord,' replied Teutorix.

'We will need to construct new wooden shields at least five feet tall so we can gain maximum protection.'

'They will be very heavy to bear my lord.'

'I have no doubt,' replied Odo, 'but the two men carrying them will be the strongest in my band.'

'I will see to it lord,' replied Teutorix.

Arni gazed enquiringly at Odo. 'I'm guessing I will be one of the men?'

'You and Sagtha, this will be a chance for him to redeem himself,' said Odo.

'How do we go about engaging their attention? The full moon has passed and it's not as if we can invite them to join us,' sneered Ingvar.

'That is something for us to ponder,' replied Odo quietly. 'Brother will you ask Aun to attend us?'

The wiry rune master joined the men shortly afterwards. Odo explained their dilemma.

'Aun, we need your insight into how we can lure these demons to their destruction. Can you cast your stones and see if they indicate a path we can follow?'

'It will take more than runes, my lord, to show us the way. A sacrifice provides the ultimate oracle, particularly a human sacrifice. A young Celtic boy would do,' suggested Aun hopefully.

'Make a sacrifice if you wish but there will be no human sacrifice Aun,' responded Odo wearily.

'I will see what the stones show me, my lord,' said

Aun.

Aun retreated to a clearing in some trees beside the settlement and began to construct a small tent of animal skins over a wooden frame with an opening at its top. When it was complete he retreated inside, lit a fire and began to chant in a sing song voice. The smoke that emanated from the tent was dense and held a peculiarly sweet smell.

After an hour he emerged staggering with glassy eyes and holding onto a small bag which he placed on the ground. He sat down cross legged beside the bag, opened it and extracted a number of small, smooth flat pebbles which he laid out in a pattern. These he moved around, all the while singing to himself. The faces of the pebbles were blank.

When he had the pebbles to his liking he began to turn them over. Each pebble held a different symbol. When all the symbols were face up Aun studied the order of them intently for a long time. He then gathered them up, put them back in the bag and retreated into the tent. He didn't emerge until the early evening at which point he walked down to the beach, removed his clothing and plunged into the sea. He surfaced and waded back to the shore where he dried himself and put his tunic back on.

He found Odo and the others sitting around an open fire inside the settlement over which a haunch of mutton was roasting.

'Have you something to tell us?' asked Odo.

'I have my lord, but first I must eat.'

'Bodvar, serve Aun first,' commanded Odo.

When Aun had eaten his fill and drunk from a wooden goblet of wine he began to speak.

'I see death my lord, the possibility of failure, abandonment, the loss of control. It will take courage, a test of faith, no empty handed leap into the void, a test of the limits to which we can drive ourselves, something we cannot avoid,' he paused for breath and sipped some wine.

'What nonsense is this,' muttered Ingvar under his breath but loud enough for Odo to hear.

'Patience Ingvar,' admonished Odo quietly.

'A boy will show us the path. He, alone, has the ability to penetrate the depths where the creatures lurk. He will be the bait that will lure them to their destruction should Odin permit it. The essence is water and this boy is good in the water. I see now why he came among us.'

Aun stopped speaking and burst out in a cackling laughing.

'Should he fail he will become their sacrifice. To think I did not see that. Odin may have his sacrifice after all.' He then relapsed into silence.

'Who is this boy?' asked Thorvald gently.

Aun rocked back and forth where he sat with an idiotic grin on his face.

'Siegfried, of course, he alone has the power of nemesis, either theirs or his,' at which point he cackled again.

'But where are these demons to be found?' asked Odo.

Aun waved an arm in the direction of the sea. 'They can be found in a deep pool on a rocky isle off the coast.'

'Which isle?' asked Odo.

'Teutorix knows,' he replied, at which point he stood up and left the group of men around the fire.

Odo, Thorvald, Arni and Ingvar looked at one another. Arni was the first to break the silence.

'Siegfried has done enough. I, for one, would not like to place him in danger again.'

'We may not have to,' said Odo, 'if what Aun says is true. Let us first locate this isle and see what it holds. Tomorrow we will question Teutorix.'

Chapter Twenty Four

Odo sat next to Teutorix and asked him what he knew about any local islands.

'There are three small islands some way off the coast. The fishermen avoid them as they believe they are cursed and more than one fisherman has never returned from there.'

'Sounds like it could be what we are looking for,' said Odo. 'Can you organise two fishing boats to take me and some of my men there and several of the largest fishing nets they have?'

'No fisherman will take you there,' replied Teutorix.

Odo laughed. 'We are not land lubbers Teutorix. We can find our own way once we know the direction.'

Teutorix organised two fishing boats for Odo and a handful of his men. His smith had been busy and had covered two newly made wooden shields in a thin covering of lead plus helmets and leggings. The boats would take five men each. Odo selected those to go with him including Arni, Sagtha, Siegfried and Agnar, the best sailor among them, and Rollo. If the monsters appeared his arrows would be needed. An archer had the benefit of being able to inflict damage out of range of their venomous breath. Spears were also added to the collection of weaponry the Vikings took.

Odo and Agnar also questioned two local fishermen who knew the waters around the islands.

They waited till the following day before departing. The wind was in their favour and the two boats laden with the men, their weapons and supplies set off from the shore.

Odo's last instruction had been to Thorvald.

'If we are not back within three days bring Skidbaldnir and the rest of the men to find out what has happened to us.' Thorvald nodded.

The sea was relatively calm and the fishing boats kept up a good pace as they sailed westwards in a brisk breeze.

The islands were some way off the coast and the Vikings came across them by late morning. They appeared to be nothing more than low, rocky outcrops though the largest was of some size.

Odo indicated to Agnar that they should aim for this island first.

Agnar spotted a narrow shingle beach and steered his craft towards it. The other boat followed.

As the boats ground onto the shingle beach the Vikings leapt out. Two from each boat plunged through the surf and headed for the higher ground to see what awaited them. The others reversed the boats and pulled them stern first up onto the shore.

Apart from flocks of gulls everything seemed peaceful. Odo split his men up into pairs to search the island with instructions to rendezvous back at the beach.

Hastein and Hakon ventured the most useful information.

'There is a small lake towards the south west of the island,' said Hakon, 'the water is warm on the hand.'

Odo rounded up his men and they all set off for the lake.

'This could be their lair,' said Odo.

'Siegfried, Thor knows you have proved yourself but would you be willing to dive down and take a look?'

asked Odo.

Siegfried was frightened but dare not show his nerves in front of this group of proven warriors.

'Yes, my lord, I will,' replied Siegfried.

'Good boy,' said Odo clasping his shoulder.

With a rope tied round his middle Siegfried dived gracefully into the pool and descended rapidly out of sight.

Several minutes went by before Siegfried rose to the surface and swam strongly towards the rim of the pool. He looked pale and frightened.

'They are there my lord and one attacked me.'

'What do you mean?' asked Odo.

'He opened his mouth and sent flame in my direction. It covered me but had no effect. As soon as that happened I swam back up to the surface.'

'Well done Siegfried. Now get dried and put your clothes on.'

Odo turned to his men.

'Interesting. Their breath has no effect in sea water.'

'How is that going to help us?' asked Arni.

‘I’m not sure,’ said Odo, ‘but it seems to me the ideal way to destroy them is in or under water.’

‘How do we achieve that?’ asked Arni, ‘we are not sea creatures.’

‘I don’t know,’ replied Odo.

It was a Cormorant that gave him the idea. The island abounded in Cormorants that dived into the sea and pools looking for fish.

‘We need fish,’ said Odo.

‘Agnar, take the fishing boats out to sea with some of the men and deploy some of the nets each boat contains. We need fish and plenty of them. And leave me four of the largest nets.’

‘Yes my lord,’ said a puzzled Agnar.

Odo took the nets and directed his men to join them together in one huge net hung along its centre with weights.

When the four nets were joined and weighted he explained his plan.

Arni was the one who voiced his scepticism on behalf of the others.

‘No, I don’t know whether the plan will work,’ said Odo, ‘but it’s the best I can think of at the moment’.

Odo directed his men to the edges of the pool, which, thankfully, was not very wide, and they dropped the folded net along one edge. The ends of the net were weighted down with stones along the one rim of the pond while they waited for Agnar to reappear.

Two hours later Agnar beached his boat with a happy smile on his face.

‘We had to go some way out but fish, we have more fish than you know what to do with,’ he said.

Several score of gulls and cormorants circled hungrily above the boat eying the catch.

Once the catch had been unloaded on the shore Odo directed that at least a quarter of the fish were slit open, stones inserted into them and closed up with twine.

‘Now let’s see if these demons bite,’ said Odo.

The fish in large wicker baskets were taken to edge of the pool and Odo directed his men to throw them in. The weighted fish sank swiftly while those not weighted tended to float on the surface. Once the fish were released the cormorants began to dive into the pool, some going down many feet to retrieve the sinking fish. The gulls got into the act too.

'Let's hope this bait and the birds' incursion into the water attracts those creatures,' said Odo.

As the men were carrying the fish to the pool Arni and Sagtha entered the sea until their hair and tunics were soaked with sea water. They then adorned the lead covered leggings and helmets, sliding their left arms through the lead covered shields. Both carried long two handed swords. Very few men could wield the heavy two handed swords effectively and they were not favoured by the Vikings as you went shieldless into any conflict but Odo had two in his possession, captured from Celts in Britain. Arni and Sagtha had the strength to wield them one handed. The extra length would be vital as both men would attempt to hack at the dragons from the edge of the pool, should they take the bait.

The surface of the pool was in turmoil as Cormorants and gulls attempted to retrieve the fish thrown in by the Vikings.

Odo began to get anxious as there was no sign of the monsters and the birds were harvesting the fish with deadly precision.

Arni and Sagtha had moved to opposite sides of the pool and Rollo was standing behind Odo and the rest of the men on a raised outcrop of rock with his bow in his hand and his quiver full of arrows held by Siegfried who would pass them to him one at a time once he started shooting.

Just as he began to give up hope a huge shape was discernible in the water. One of the beasts at least had come up to gorge on the fish and the cormorants that were deep in the water.

Odo looked at his men who were grasping the edges of the weighted net by the edge of the pool.

'Don't move until I give you the command,' he said.

Looking into the pool Odo discerned a second shape and then a third. All three creatures were near the surface; their multiple heads seeking and devouring fish and birds alike.

'Now!' cried Odo.

The men holding the net moved swiftly along the edges of the pool to the opposite side. The net was now below the monsters and, assuming it was strong enough, it would prevent them from descending back into the depths.

'Pull!' shouted Odo.

The men who held the edges of the net all round the pool began to move outwards from the edges of the pool pulling the net with them.

The effect of this manoeuvre was to bring fish, birds and monsters to the surface of the pool as the net was now suspended only a few feet below the surface of the water. Caught in the netting were the three beasts; confused and angry.

Rollo began to shoot his arrows at the bodies he could see. His arrows appeared to have little effect other than to inflame the creatures who began to shriek loudly. He switched his aim to their heads. Siegfried was passing arrows as quickly as possible to Rollo.

One monster reared up and lurched towards the side of the pond where Sagtha was standing. His three heads held at least one arrow each. As the heads came within range Sagtha swung his sword and lopped off one head. On the reverse swing he chopped off another. The third head swung in his direction and fixed him with two red baleful eyes before opening its jaws and spitting a jet of yellow vapour at him. Sagtha moved his shield quickly and it caught the full blast of the breath. As his breath died away Sagtha found he was still alive and in one piece. He risked a look over the edge of his shield seeking a chance to swing his sword at the remaining head.

On the other side of the pond Arni waited for his opportunity to strike at the other two dragons should they come within range.

Odo had not been idle. Grasping several spears he had set off to stand behind Arni to attempt to lure at least one of the beasts in Arni's direction. He took a firm grip on his first spear and cast it at the nearest beast. It found its mark. He followed up by throwing two more. The beast saw the direction the spears were coming from and lunged across the surface of the water towards

Odo and Arni sending gouts of yellow vapour towards them.

Once the heads were in range of Arni's sword he didn't hesitate. With two blows he sheared two of the heads off the beast who kept coming. With a third blow Arni finished the job and the monster shuddered and toppled onto its side. Sagtha meanwhile, had succeeded in chopping off the third head of the already incapacitated beast. This left the remaining monster to deal with who remained in the relative safety of the centre of the pool.

Odo acted quickly and commanded the men on the far side of the pool to raise the edge of the net they were holding and to work their way towards where he and Arni were standing. This had the effect of enveloping the dragon within the folds of the net who began to direct his vapour at the net directly. This began to cause large holes to appear in the netting. But the holes were not big enough for the monster to escape. The Vikings by sheer brute strength dragged the remaining reptile towards the edge of the pond where

Arni and Sagtha were now waiting with their swords held at the ready. It ended swiftly when between them they managed to separate the three heads from the beast.

The Vikings let the net go and the bodies of the beasts gradually subsided along with the net into the depths of the pool.

'Well done men,' said Odo, 'that was hard work and we will look forward to a hearty meal at Calliges expense this evening, not to mention the gold he promised us.'

At this the men raised a cheer shaking their fists in the air.

The men boarded the fishing boats and began the journey back to the mainland; Agnar leading the way.

It was close to evening when they landed and Teoutorix and a handful of men were there to greet them.

'What news my lord?' asked Teutorix anxiously.

'The deed is done,' said Odo. 'Your folk have no need to fear anymore. We killed three of the beasts and I fancy that was all of them.'

The men on the shore gave up a great cheer.

'We will feast well tonight,' promised Teutorix, 'and I will send word to Calliges'.

The lady Nevena was waiting among those on the shore and couldn't restrain herself from rushing into Odo's arms.

'I was worried my lord. I thought I may not see you and the others again.'

'Hush now lady. It will take more than a handful of beasts to get the better of me and the men here,' said a slightly embarrassed Odo.

The lady Nevena slipped her hand into his and with the rest of the men they made their way back to the settlement.

The dinner was as fine as any the Vikings could recall. The pork and crackling were delicious; the wine smoother than that which they had been consuming up to that point and the settlement's cook produced an array of sweetmeats which the Vikings had not experienced before. The evening ended with music and story telling.

With the moon high in the sky the Vikings settled down for the night though Odo posted a rotating watch through the night.

Nevena asked Odo whether this was necessary.

'It always pays to be cautious my lady. That's why I am still alive while others I know are now in Valhalla.'

And please call me Nevena. We can dispense with formal titles after what we have been through together.'

'Yes my lady, I mean Nevena.'

The lady Nevena took him by the hand and together they entered a hut that had been set aside for her.

'You will sleep here tonight with me,' she commanded.

Odo did not object. He was dog tired and fell asleep within minutes. Nevena looked at him lovingly as she brushed the hair from his face.

Chapter Twenty Five

The following morning Calliges arrived with his household warriors.

'You have done me and the Redones a valuable service,' said Calliges. 'Here is the gold I promised you and should you ever need my sword send word and I and my men will come wherever you may be.'

Calliges grasped Odo by the arm and then walked with him towards the beach where Skidbladnir was being loaded ready for the journey across the channel to Britain.

'Where lies your destiny now?' asked Calliges.

'My first duty is to return the lady Nevena to her people. After that only Odin knows what is in store for me and my men.'

Siegfried was saying goodbye to Teutorix. He had come to like the slim but effective warrior and was determined to gain a similar mastery of the sword.

'Find yourself a good teacher, two swords and who knows one day you may be a warrior to reckon with,' said Teutorix, 'you have the speed, reflexes and the potential.'

The Vikings boarded their longship and Agnar set a course for Britain. The wind was favourable coming from the south west as it was. Once clear of the bay the Vikings ceased their rowing and the large sail billowed in the stiff breeze.

They crossed the channel without incident and Agnar had plotted their course accurately so that as Britain came into view they recognised the wide estuary that led to Siegfried's home settlement.

'Why so glum boy?' asked Arni on seeing Siegfried's downcast demeanour.

'I'm worried about what my father and mother will say on my return. I feel guilty at having left them without saying goodbye. But one thing I know is that I do not want to be a farmer. I want to be a warrior and stay with you.'

Siegfried had grown and hardened in his time with the Viking band and now sported two gold arm rings given him by Odo for his bravery and deeds.

'Our lord will speak with your father and I'm sure the

outcome will be positive. Besides, with your share of gold and silver from Calliges, and what is owed us by Caderyn, you have more than enough to be independent. You have the resources to determine your own path,' said Arni.

As they entered the estuary the wind dropped and the men took to their oars.

It was an easy row to the Regni village and by late afternoon the longship arrived opposite the settlement and pulled into the pier that extended into the river.

Awaiting the Vikings on the shore was Drustan with his ten warriors, armed in case the longship was not Skidbladnir or had been taken over by others whose intent may not be peaceful.

Drustan recognised Odo with relief and welcomed him and the others ashore.

'You have been gone many days,' said Drustan by way of greeting, 'we were concerned that the Dumnonii or the Durotriges had got the better of you.'

'As you see we are all well and we have the lady Nevena with us,' said Odo.

'The gods be praised,' replied Drustan, 'our high lord Cadeyrn will be pleased. I will send word to him at once. But tonight you will recount your adventures in our hall.'

'Not another feast,' muttered Odo to Arni in Norse, 'the men will get too used to this and become fat and lazy.'

'I don't know about you, but I'm looking forward to a hearty meal and some beer instead of what passes for drink in Gaul. Beats the hard tack on board any day,' said Arni with a twinkle in his eye.

The evening was spent merrily in the company of the Regni with Skorri recounting their adventures in a lilting sing song tone.

Cadeyrn and his hearth troop arrived mid-morning the following day. He was delighted to see his sister and to hear about what transpired among the Dumnonii, though he was concerned at the political ramifications arising out of Odo's expedition along with the effect it had on the Dumnonii's allies, the Durotriges.

Odo, naturally, was less concerned.

'We have rid the Dumonii of an evil witch and two of

her monsters and brought the lady Nevena home safe and sound.' said Odo, 'I cannot think the Prince of Tormorhun will be much of a threat to you in the future.'

'That may be true my lord Odo, but the Durotriges, on behalf of the Prince of Tormorhun, have put a price on your head and I would steer clear of their territory. Once word reaches them that you have arrived within my domain I fear they will send a raiding party for you. They are always looking for an excuse to fight the Regni. It is with a heavy heart that I must ask you to leave our lands. I cannot risk the wrath they will bring down on this settlement or any other. Drustan is a good man and a capable warrior but he and his men are not enough to hold them at bay and I have troubles in the north to deal with where I and my men are needed.'

Odo, who had hoped to spend the winter among the Regni, was not happy at this turn of events. He had wanted to see more of Nevena and for the first time harboured a vision of settling down in this land which was fertile and green with an equable climate, compared to the harsh environment of his homeland.

'I will grant you a week before you must set forth. And, before I forget, I have something for you,' he said indicating a heavy looking chest that one of his men had set at his feet.

'This is the reward we agreed and should go some way towards recompensing you for not being able to enjoy our continued hospitality,' said Cadeyrn.

'I appreciate that my lord,' replied Odo.

'Now, I must be away,' said Cadeyrn, 'Nevena, where are you? We leave soon.'

The lady Nevena had been watching the exchange between her brother and Odo and now came forward.

'I shall not be coming with you brother. I owe these Vikings my life and I would stay with them for the coming week at least.'

Cadeyrn frowned but saw the set look on her face and knew how hard it was to change her sister's mind when it was made up.

'I shall leave four men here to escort you back once the Vikings have departed,' said Cadeyrn brusquely.

'Thank you brother,' said Nevena.

At that Cadeyrn turned away and stalked off calling for his men to ready themselves for departure.

Siegfried had gone home with trepidation but his mother and father were overjoyed at seeing him again and at how much he had grown. They didn't refer to his abscondment, though his sister told him later that their father had been furious when he had found out.

'I'm sure the experience was character forming Siegfried and now you have returned there is much to do before winter sets in,' said his father.

Siegfried nodded, not having the heart to tell him that when the Vikings left he would go with them. There was time enough for that in the coming days.

Nevana and Odo walked along the river and stopped to look at some children splashing in the shallows.

Nevena turned towards Odo and rested both her hands on his arms.

'My lord, I have come to a decision. I will not be returning to Cadeyrn's hearth. There is nothing there for me. I will miss Cadeyrn, Badeyrn and our family but I won't miss the politics and the usual intrigue that accompanies their court. I want my future to be with you wherever that may be.'

'We have no settled home,' replied Odo, 'all I can promise you is danger and the unknown. That is no place for a lady like you.'

'My home is with you, Thorvald, Arni and the others. I have never felt so alive since I have been in your company and you cannot fail to have noticed the love I have for you. Unless you forbid it, my mind is made up and I will be coming with you,' said Nevena firmly. 'I may not be a warrior, though the gods know I can wield a sword when I have to, and I can cook and sew. And as a priestess of the druids I have knowledge of healing and certain powers which may prove useful.'

Odo saw the defiance in her face and nodded.

'So be it. I was hoping that you might join us,' said Odo grinning.

Nevena burst out laughing and gave him a big hug.

'But there is a condition,' said Odo seriously.

Nevena looked at him, suddenly worried.

'You have to help me persuade Siegfried's parents

that he has no desire to become a farmer and that he wishes to travel with us. I'm sure it will be a comfort to them to know that you will help look after him while he grows into full manhood.'

'Of course I will, said Nevena relieved.

The conversation with Siegfried's parents was not easy but Odo, Nevena and Arni promised they would look after Siegfried and said that he would be perfectly safe in their company. They pointed out that he was a natural warrior. Siegfried also decided to leave the bulk of his newly acquired wealth with them to invest in their small holding; more gold and silver than his father had earnt in his lifetime.

Siegfried's father knew about destiny, having left Britain for Gaul many years before, and knew that this was the path the gods had chosen for Siegfried and that it would not be right to prevent him leaving. Siegfried had chosen his path as all young men had to do.

The week passed and the day soon came when the Vikings boarded their longship for the journey downriver and back out onto the open sea.

Drustan was apologetic about the fact they had to leave and despite Cadeyrns' instruction insisted that should they ever need a safe haven then they could return at any time and would be made welcome.

As the longship eased down river Siegfried stood at the stern with Nevena waving goodbye and watching the figures of his family and the other villagers slowly recede into the distance.

Siegfried had tears in his eyes as did Nevena.

Nevena put an arm round Siegfried.

'Whatever the gods have in store for us,' she said, 'I'm sure we have made the right decision.'

'I know we have,' said Siegfried smiling.

Historical Note

Siegfried and the Vikings is a mythical story set in ancient Britain in 100 BC. The Celtic tribes mentioned – the Regnii, Atrebates, Duritoges, Dumnoii, Ordovices, Redones - did exist as did the druids.

The earliest known records show that Vikings appeared in Britain in the 790s AD but for the purposes of this tale I have assumed that Vikings existed long before and did visit Britain in the years before 790.

www.blossomspringpublishing.com

Printed in Poland
by Amazon Fulfillment
Poland Sp. z o.o., Wrocław

60777739R10200